Delta-Victor

Clare Revell

Delta-Victor

Cover Art by Nicola Martinez

Watershed Books, a division of Pelican Ventures, LLC
www.pelicanbookgroup.com PO Box 1738 *Aztec, NM * 87410

Watershed Books praise and splash logo is a trademark of Pelican Ventures, LLC

Publishing History
First Watershed Edition, 2015
Paperback Edition ISBN 978-1-61116-507-4
Electronic Edition ISBN 978-1-61116-506-7
Published in the United States of America

Dedication

For Rhys, Ceryn, and Jess.
My three angels.

1

The daylight grew, the warm sun illuminating the beach and their makeshift campsite. Sixteen-year-old Lou Benson woke and for the life of her, couldn't work out where she was. She was cold and stiff and her injured leg hurt. She sat up and looked around. Why would they camp on a beach with no blankets, when they had nice warm beds on board their boat, *Avon*?

Deefer, her golden and white Sheltie, rubbed his nose against her face in greeting and she petted him. "Hey, boy. Guess there's no point asking you why we're here, is there?"

He barked and shook his head.

Lou looked out across the bay. No boat. Where was it? Then she remembered. They were shipwrecked.

A wave of fear and sadness swept over her. She felt incredibly cold, almost as if the sun had been blotted out or removed from the sky altogether. This was her fault. The whole mess was her fault.

Jim Kirk rolled onto his side and opened his eyes. He smiled at her and she wished her heart would stop that double beat thing. He was a friend, nothing more, and never would be. Her best friend she'd given up everything to help.

"So much for a rescue trip to find your parents," she said quietly.

His clear eyes clouded for a moment. "The rescuers need rescuing," he said. "If I hadn't fallen asleep at the helm..."

Lou shifted uncomfortably. "It wasn't your fault. Stuff happens."

Before he could say anything further, his younger sister, Staci, rolled over and sat. She stretched, looking confused as she brushed the sand off her arms. "Where are we?" she asked. "And don't say camping, because I can see that."

"Agrihan."

"Oh, I remember now." Staci looked at the few bags by their feet. "We didn't save much, did we? And I left the laptop behind."

Jim took hold of his sister's hand and gave it a comforting squeeze. "There wasn't time, kiddo."

Lou reached into her sewing bag and pulled out the camera. "Let's have one for the record," she said. "Our first camp-out." She took the photo and put the camera away. "At least we posted all those discs back to Mum and stuck some of the photos on the web. So we'll still have the pictures."

"Sorry I forgot the laptop," Staci said.

Jim rummaged through the food bag. "Stop apologizing for forgetting the laptop. We all got off before *Avon* sank. Nothing else matters. Are sandwiches all right for breakfast?"

"Why are you never hungry on the beach?"

Staci asked.

Jim shook his head. "Don't know."

"Because of all the sand which is there." Lou told him.

He rolled his eyes. "I see you two still haven't lost your sense of humor."

"I see you still haven't found yours," Lou retorted.

Jim scowled. "You guys just don't get it, do you? We're shipwrecked. There is no way off here."

Lou sighed. "Lighten up, Jim. We may be down, but we are not out."

"There has to be a settlement somewhere on this island right?" Staci said. "They're bound to have phones. Everyone does these days. We can get help there. Now breakfast. We'd better go easy on the food. It may take us a while to find help." She looked at Jim. "We are in this together. Strength and honor, right?"

Jim looked up. "I guess so. It's just we were meant to be searching for Mum and Dad and now we're lost, too."

"We know. But there isn't much we can do sat here," Staci said. "We need to find help. That means not sitting here feeling sorry for ourselves, but having breakfast, getting off our butts, and going to look for a village." She paused. "Wait a minute. When did I suddenly become the grown up around here?"

"When Jim decided to act like a ten-year-old," Lou replied. "He's the only grown up I can see for mi—" She winked. "Well, on this beach actually."

Deefer barked in agreement.

Jim nodded slowly. "You're right. As usual." He made breakfast and they ate quietly. Deefer finished his and wanted more.

Jim looked at him. "Sorry, mate, you can't. We have to make it last."

After they had all finished, Lou packed away the rubbish, while Staci put the rest of the stuff away.

Jim put sand over the extinguished fire to ensure it wouldn't re-light.

Lou put on one of the rucksacks and Staci the other.

Jim put the holdall across his chest and shouldered Lou's sewing bag. He clipped Deefer's lead on and looked at the others. "Are you ready then?"

"Willing and able," they chorused.

"Then let's go."

Jim led the way into the forest and down a path, which was really nothing more than a sandy trail with a deep groove in the center.

Lou's crutches sank into the sand, making keeping up nigh on impossible with the fast pace Jim set. She trailed behind, barely taking her eyes off the path. Her leg hurt and she didn't dare put any weight on it. It was one thing hobbling around a boat on crutches, doing it on unfamiliar territory was another problem altogether.

The trees towered over them, offering shade from the blazing heat of the sun. It was only ten in the morning, but already the temperature was in the high seventies. The sandy path beneath her feet finally turned to dried mud.

Above them in the trees birds sang, parrots squawked and leaves rustled. In any other circumstances, Lou would have enjoyed the walk. She loved exploring and wanted to be an archeologist when she left school.

As it was, she could think of a dozen other things she'd much rather be doing.

Even on the dried mud path, keeping up was difficult. The ground was uneven and the path was well worn and dipped in the middle.

She kept losing her footing on the unstable ground. After an hour's walking, she could barely see the others in front of her, although she could still hear Staci chattering.

Lou stumbled, crying out as pain shot up her leg. The fragile tissue started to give. It had never really healed since the shark attack several weeks ago. She sat on the ground, cradling her leg and blinking back tears.

Jim stopped and came back to her. "Are you all right?"

"Do I look all right?" she snapped. Then she sucked in a deep breath. This wasn't Jim's fault. "Sorry. I slipped. I could do with a rest."

"OK. It looks a bit clearer just up ahead, and I can hear water. Can you go on a bit farther?"

The thought filled her with dread, but she wasn't going to say as much. They had to find civilization and get help. "So long as it isn't too far. This is farther than I've walked in weeks."

"It isn't far, I promise." Jim helped her up,

returned to the head of the line, and set off again.

Staci glanced over her shoulder. "This is like playing Brown's Cows. Remember that?"

Lou grinned. "Oh yeah, drove Mum mad with it." They'd followed her mother around the flat in a line for over an hour. Until she'd decided enough was enough and made them sit down. "Not as much fun as hanging pegs on the back on her skirt."

Staci giggled. "I'd forgotten that. She even went to church with them still attached."

Five minutes later they came into a clearing. A stream meandered to the left of it, bubbling over the rocks, and the sun blazed through the gap in the tree cover.

Lou limped over to a fallen log and gingerly sat. She put her crutches down, rubbed her leg and dropped the rucksack. "It's nice to sit," she sighed.

Staci put her rucksack on the ground and sat next to Lou. "Sure is," she agreed. "It's hard keeping up with Jim. I don't know where he gets his energy from. Nichola would insist on bottling it and making a fortune by selling it."

Jim crossed to the stream. He squatted beside it and scooped up a handful. He tasted it and turned to the girls. "Tastes fine." He pulled empty bottles from his pack and filled them with water. Next, he filled cups and carried them to the girls.

Lou fished out a bowl and gave it to Jim, who filled it for Deefer.

After they'd rested a bit, Jim stood. "I suggest we follow the stream. Most villages are built close to water. It's our best chance of finding help."

"But the path goes that way," Staci pointed. "Lou would find it easier to follow the path."

"Maybe, but our best bet for finding help is the stream."

"Path," Staci insisted. "It's well used, and the chances are we'll meet someone on it."

Lou held up her hand. "Guys, please. There is no point in arguing. I can't go anywhere. Not for a while, anyway." She didn't need a mirror to know she looked as pale as she felt.

"Are you OK?" Jim asked, concerned. "You look dreadful."

"Good, dreadful is how I want to look." She couldn't resist trying to get one over on him. If nothing else it'd divert Staci's attention from how bad things really were. "Seriously, I've been better. I've just overdone it a bit. How about I stay here with Staci and you go exploring with Deefer. That way you won't get lost."

"OK. I'll check the stream out," Jim said. He called Deefer, and the two of them set off.

~*~

He had to admit, it was tough going. What originally had looked like a path very soon vanished. He pushed his way through waist high grass and thick undergrowth.

Deefer whined his disapproval.

Jim looked down at him. "Staci was right. Lou would never manage this. We'd better try the path." Jim struck off to his right. The trees were

Clare Revell

less dense that way.

When he reached a path he stopped. He should have back tracked. "Question is, is it the same one?"

He turned to his left and followed the path. Deefer, tail wagging now, ran on ahead and out of sight.

"Deefer?" Jim called. "Deefer, where are you? Lou will never forgive me if something happens to you."

Deefer started barking.

"Deefer?" Jim pushed through the brush, shoved back a curtain of leaves, and stopped in amazement. "Wow! Would you look at that?"

2

Back at the stream, Staci shook Lou awake.

Lou looked at her sleepily. "What's up? Is Jim back?"

"No. He's been gone almost four hours. I'm worried."

"He's got Deefer with him. He'll be fine. Tell you what, if you do something to eat, he's bound to come back."

"OK. It'll have to be sandwiches as I can't light a fire."

"Jim's better at that sort of thing," Lou said, settling back to watch Staci get more water from the stream to dilute the juice. Lou yawned and rubbed her leg. She and Staci had barely taken their first bites when Jim and Deefer came into the clearing.

"Told you," Lou grinned.

Jim flopped down beside them. "Lunch," he said. "I'm starving. You should see what we found."

"Is that the royal we?" Lou asked. "Or is it just delusions of grandeur on your part?"

"Me and Deefer."

"Deefer and I," she corrected.

"Oh, pssht." Not even her teasing could

diminish his enthusiasm or the grin on his face. Whatever he'd found had to be pretty spectacular. "It's amazing."

"Did you find civilization?" Staci asked.

"Not exactly, but signs thereof. It's a temple. Albeit a slightly dilapidated one, but it means there are people here somewhere."

"How far?"

"About forty minutes down the path." Jim paused. "Well, probably more like an hour and a half at Lou's speed. There's water so we need only take enough for the journey. We could stay there tonight."

After they finished lunch, Staci rinsed the cups and knife in the stream and, once again, topped up the water bottles.

Then they set off up the path in search of Jim's temple. It took them just over the hour and a half that Jim had estimated.

Lou limped as slowly as she could. She was in a great deal of pain from her shark-damaged leg, more so than usual, but was trying not to let it show. "Where's this temple then?" she asked as they entered the clearing.

"Here," Jim answered pulling aside the leafy curtain covering the offshoot of the path.

Staci and Lou went through and stopped in wonder.

Before them rose the remains of an ornate building. Huge pillars supported the roof. Creepers entwined themselves around the pillars adding to the ethereal charm. Stone steps rose from the ground up to the entrance. Flowers and leaves were carved around the tops of the pillars while some kind of bird was carved into the base.

"There's more inside," Jim told them. "The windows give enough light for us to see. The roof has gone in a couple of places, but there's plenty of shelter."

Lou struggled over to the steps and sank down wearily. "You two explore. I'll catch up in a bit. Take the camera and get some photos."

As the others disappeared inside, she rubbed her leg and grimaced as the pain increased.

Deefer sat down next to her and whined.

She patted the top of his head. "Just wish I had the energy to go look for myself. It's an archeologist's dream."

~*~

Inside the temple, Staci looked around, fascinated. "It's nothing like any ruins I've ever seen. There's no dust or debris. It looks well cared for despite the holes in the roof and walls."

"Look at this," Jim said. He pointed to one of the walls. It was divided into panels. Tiny pictures and some kind of writing covered each panel.

Staci ran her fingers over them. "Are they hiro, hero...oh, those glyph things?"

"Hieroglyphics? Yes, I think so. They obviously tell some kind of story, but I don't know what."

Staci said, "Are we staying here tonight?"

"Yes. We might need to help Lou up the

steps. Is she OK? She's very quiet."

"She's walked farther today than she has for weeks."

Jim shrugged. "Yeah, but we all have."

"Yes, but not on crutches. She's also in a lot more pain than she's letting on. We'll have to take things a lot easier tomorrow. Maybe just move on every other day."

Jim went back to the temple entrance. He went down the steps.

Lou was hunched over at the bottom of them.

"Lou?"

She looked up, rubbing her eyes with her sleeve. "I'm here."

Jim pushed aside a touch of embarrassment at having caught her off guard and sat next to her, concern flooding him. "Are you all right?" he asked gently.

She nodded. "I'm fine."

"Liar. You're not fine at all, because normally you'd be jumping through hoops to explore this place. Is the pain really bad?"

"I've just over done it," Lou gasped, her face creasing as a fresh wave of pain swept over her. "I'll be OK." She looked at him. "Honestly, Jim, I'm just tired."

"We'll stay here tomorrow to give you a rest. Let's get you inside. There's something I want you to see. It might take your mind off how tired you feel for a few minutes."

"Can't see that happening, but OK. I'll come." Lou struggled to her feet and with Jim's help made it to the top of the steps. She gripped her crutches and limped inside the temple after him.

Staci had found some cloth in a box. "It's weird," she said, showing them. "This looks almost new. So does the box."

Lou studied the symbols on the wall. "These pictographs are amazing. They tell the story of the building of the temple and what happened to the people who built it."

"You can read them?" Jim asked in astonishment.

Lou smiled. "Misspent youth," she replied.

Jim laughed. "I'm sorry? I thought you were only sixteen. I forgot for a minute you turned fifty a couple of months ago."

Lou poked her tongue at him. "Ha, ha. Very funny. You know I find the whole archaeology thing fascinating. I've spent hours studying Egyptian and Mayan hieroglyphics and pictographs. Apparently some kind of disaster struck the people shortly before the temple was begun. As a result the temple took a many years to complete."

"What happened?"

"I'll need a lot longer to study them if you want the whole story." She crossed over to one of the statues. "This guy looks familiar."

"It's Jim." Staci said.

Lou laughed. "It does look like him, doesn't it? No seriously. I know this guy, but I can't, for the life of me, remember his name."

"So until you remember, we'll just call him Jim." Staci laughed.

Jim rolled his eyes. "Thank you."

"You're welcome."

Lou turned and her leg gave out. She dropped the crutches and toppled to the floor, crying out as she fell.

Jim dashed across to her. "You OK?"

"Yeah, I'm fine. It's just this stupid leg. Help me up, please."

Jim pulled her upright.

Staci passed her the crutches.

Lou looked at them. "Honestly, I'm fine. Just tired."

"I found some cushions as well," Staci said. "You can rest properly tonight. I'll show you."

"It's half five," Jim said. "I'll get a fire going outside for tea, shall I?"

"Please. I'll get Lou settled, and I'll be there."

Lou sank onto the cushions and closed her eyes. She could control the pain better like this. A thud on her chest and a heavy sigh told her Deefer was using her as a pillow again. She took a couple of deep breaths as she stroked his ears. "Maybe I'll remember where I've seen the statue before, when I'm not so tired," she told him.

Deefer licked her hand.

Staci giggled. "I think that was him agreeing with you. I'm going to see what Jim's doing."

Lou waved a hand. "Sure, Deefer and I will lie here and think about statues."

~*~

Jim came to tell Lou tea was ready, and

found her asleep. He returned out to Staci. "She's asleep. I won't wake her."

"What about tea?"

"We'll have to eat it. We can't keep it warm, can we?"

"True."

Jim divided Lou's between them.

Deefer ate his and disappeared back inside to Lou.

Staci looked at Jim. "Is there any way we can have a fire inside?"

"Not really. I thought I might light one of those torches later when it gets dark."

They lapsed into silence and finished tea.

Staci rinsed the dishes in the stream. Then she and Jim sat by the fire and watched the stars come out as darkness fell. Before the fire died completely, Jim carried a piece of blazing wood inside and lit two of the torches in the room where Lou was sleeping.

Jim rejoined Staci on the steps of the temple. He pointed out the constellations to her. There were many they didn't usually see in England, but most of them were the same, just in different places in the night sky.

Staci yawned. "I'm tired." She looked around. "Where's Deefer?"

"With Lou."

"I should've known," Staci laughed. "I'm going to bed. You coming?"

"In a bit."

Staci rose. "'Night."

Jim watched her go. He'd explore tomorrow

while Lou took it easy. He took a last look at the stars and walked inside.

Both the girls slept.

Deefer raised his head and wagged his tail in greeting.

Jim patted him and Deefer settled again.

Jim sat on his blanket. He wished he knew what to do and where to go. Of course, there was One who did. Closing his eyes, he began to pray. He'd messed up in the biggest way possible, and didn't deserve any help trying to put it right and get the girls to safety. But then, he hadn't deserved his salvation either. He wasn't asking God to solve the problem, just to guide him in what to do next.

3

The next morning they were woken just after seven by Deefer barking.

Lou sat up and put her hand on his collar. "Shush."

Deefer shook himself loose and went to the doorway. He stiffened and growled.

Jim got to his feet and motioned to the girls to be quiet. He picked up a stick, and hefting it in his hand, went towards the doorway.

Deefer tried to go outside with him.

Jim stopped him. "Deefer, stay here with Lou. Stay."

Deefer went obediently over to Lou and sat.

Jim crept out through the door and vanished from sight.

Deefer growled once and then fell silent.

The few minutes Jim was gone seemed to last forever. Footsteps echoed across the chamber.

Lou looked at Deefer. He was wagging his tail.

"It's all right, it's me," Jim called as he came in. "Nothing there," he reported. "But there was. Some of the grass is flattened."

"Couldn't it have been us yesterday?" Staci

asked.

"Possibly, but I doubt it. We didn't drop this anyway." He tossed Lou a gold amulet.

She caught it and turned it over. "Wow." she said. "This is gorgeous."

Staci looked at the gold carving in Lou's hand. "What is it?" she asked. "Other than a bracelet of some kind."

"It's an amulet. It's supposed to protect the wearer from evil. This is beautiful. The craftsmanship is incredible." Lou held it up to look at it more closely.

On one side was a very intricate pattern, which seemed to make no sense at all—just lines radiating out from a central point. On the other side was a bird.

"Bird," Lou said. She glanced over at the line of statues, which included a bird. "Bird. Oh, come on, woman. Think."

Jim smiled at her. "Hey, I didn't *really* expect you to know."

Lou pulled a face. "No, I've seen it. I read something at school—private study."

"That's designed for homework you know."

"We don't get private study like you did. I used to spend lunch times in the library in the archaeology section. I've seen this, but I can't remember where."

"Never mind. It means there is a village around here somewhere. I'll go and explore after breakfast. You stay here and rest, Lou."

"I'm not going to argue."

Staci pulled out the last of the bread and they

ate in silence.

When they had finished, Jim rose to his feet. "I'm off to find this village. I'll be back with help later."

"Are you taking the dog?" Staci asked.

"Not this time. He can stay with you. See you later." He waved and disappeared outside.

Lou rose. "I might go and have a look at those statues. Try and get my mind working." She limped into the inner chamber, which she hadn't been into yesterday. She wandered around slowly.

There were more statues there, including a huge one of the bird, the same as the one on the amulet. Its wings were outstretched as if it were swooping in to protect its young.

Lou clucked in exasperation. She knew this, why couldn't she remember? She went back into the chamber they had slept in.

Staci wasn't there.

Lou headed slowly to the entrance of the temple and found Staci sitting on the steps in the sunshine.

Jim came up the path.

"That was quick," Lou said.

"Been gone two hours. It's half nine," Jim told her. "There's a village about a mile from here. Shall we go?"

"I thought we were resting today?" Staci asked.

"We can do that in the village. Come on."

Lou whistled to Deefer, but he didn't come. "Deefer," she called. "Dee-fer." Lou glanced around. "Where's the silly animal gone now? Help me down these steps, will you, please?"

Jim did so.

At the bottom Lou yelled, "Deefer. Come here, now." Still nothing.

"He's probably just wandered off for a sec. He'll be back," Jim said.

A spear flew out of the bushes and landed upright in the ground in front of Staci. She screamed and jumped backwards.

Another one landed next to Jim. He froze.

And yet another thudded by Lou's feet.

All three were thrown with deadly accuracy, landing a fraction of an inch from where they each stood.

"Jim?" Staci began.

"It's OK, kiddo." Jim said, taking her hand.

More spears landed around them, completely blocking their path.

Two faces peered out at them. Both had some kind of markings on their foreheads.

They look like willow people. Lou didn't have time to process information about their customs.

"Where's Deefer?" Staci asked.

"He can take care of himself," Jim said. "We've got more important things to worry about now."

More faces appeared. Six men climbed out of the bushes and walked towards them. They all had long hair. They wore trousers and a sleeveless tunic, which hung open over bare chests. Each also wore a headband and an amulet like Jim had found. They all had the markings on their foreheads, which Lou could now tell was a tattoo.

Willow people.

One of the men spoke. He seemed angry and gesticulated wildly.

Jim shook his head and spread his hands. "I don't understand." He repeated it in Spanish.

The man spoke again. This time his tone was louder and angrier.

Jim shook his head. "What I would give for a universal translator right now. It sounds similar to Spanish, but not quite."

Footsteps came from behind them. Three more men stood, blocking them in.

Jim immediately raised his hands in surrender. "OK, I think this might be a good idea now."

Lou nodded. "'Cept I can't raise mine."

Staci raised hers, only to have them pulled behind her and tied.

Jim's hands were tugged roughly behind his back and tied them together. "Hey, there is no need for this. Let us go."

The leader spoke angrily again. He pointed at the temple. Another began to remove the spears.

"I think we upset them, somehow," Lou said. "Not a good start. Maybe the temple wasn't such a good place to camp."

One of the men picked up their bags.

Another took hold of Lou.

She lost her balance and accidentally knocked him with her crutches.

He yelped in pain.

"I'm sorry. It was an accident," Lou said.

Another man snatched her crutches away and Lou immediately fell to the ground.

Jim tried to go to her defense, but was held firmly. "She can't walk without them," he said. He repeated it in Spanish.

The leader glared at him and spoke again. He pointed at Lou.

One of the others swung her into his arms and set off down the path at a great pace.

The men behind Jim and Staci pushed them and made them follow.

The natives walked quickly.

Staci tripped and fell, unable to put her hands out to save herself. She cried out.

Without seeming to pause, a native scooped her up and carried her.

When they arrived at the village, Jim barely had time to look around before he and Staci were bundled unceremoniously into a hut. The door shut with a bang and was barred from the outside.

"Hello," Lou said. "What kept you?"

"Well, that went well," Jim said, not answering her question. "Maybe I should have packed the *What to Do When Shipwrecked for Dummies* after all."

"Actually the *What to Do When Kidnapped by Unfriendly Natives for Dummies* might have been more useful. Or the *Where Not to Camp for Dummies*." Lou paused. "Are you both OK?"

"My knee hurts," Staci said. "It's bleeding."

~*~

Jim led her into the single patch of light coming through the barred window. "It's not too bad, kiddo, just grazed." He looked out of the window. From what he could see, the village was built around a central raised dais. Rather like a cartwheel, all the buildings were in lines radiating from a central point. He looked at Lou. "The village is built like..."

"The picture on the amulet," Lou finished. "Yes. I just wish I could remember what the bird signifies or who the Jim statue really is."

Jim looked back out of the window. "There's some kind of meeting going on. All the men of the village seem to be there. No women, though."

Lou laughed. "That's our crime, then. We're women and you've been consorting with us."

"It's no laughing matter," Jim told her. "They look furious."

"Well, there is nothing we can do about it. Maybe they'll let us phone the embassy or something."

"I don't see any phone lines, do you? Or phone masts."

The morning passed slowly and the temperature rose inside the hut.

No one approached or brought them any food or water.

Jim tried shouting through the window, but that resulted in the window being shut for an hour. When it was re-opened, a welcome breeze flowed into the hut.

"Don't antagonize them again," Lou told Jim. "Hopefully one of them speaks English and all this can be worked out."

"Where are your crutches, Lou?" Staci asked.

"Same place as our bags, I imagine," Lou replied. "Just wish I knew where Deefer was. I hope he's OK."

It was midafternoon before the bar was removed from the door.

Two men came in. One carried a tray and the other stood guard at the door. He put the tray down and left without a word, barring the door behind them.

Staci picked up the tray and carried it back across to them. She pulled off the cloth covering it. "Fruit and water."

Lou took the cup she held out gratefully and sipped it. "It's not water, but it's cold. And I'm so thirsty I'd drink it anyway."

Staci looked at the fruit. "Not much choice is there?"

"Well, beggars can't be choosers." Jim picked up one of them and bit into it. "It tastes like a peach," he said.

Lou took a piece. "My favorite."

Darkness fell. Inside the hut, they could barely see. Stars shone through the small window and outside they could hear singing and drums beating. There was a fire too, as they could hear crackling and smell smoke. Soon they could smell meat roasting.

An hour later the door opened again. Another tray was brought in and the first one taken away.

Staci took the tray across to the others. "Meat, this time, and more of that drink."

Again they ate and drank in silence.

Lou wondered briefly if the food was drugged, but she was too hungry to care. A wave of tiredness swept over her. She closed her eyes. *Just a few minutes.* Her leg hurt and she was incredibly sleepy.

She came to with a jolt. There was a faint light inside the room as the full moon shone straight through the window. She moved awkwardly. "Owww."

"Hi," Jim said. "You OK?"

"Yeah. How long did I sleep?"

"Two and a half hours. It's almost midnight."

The door rattled as the bar was removed.

"What do they want now?" Lou asked.

"I take it that's a rhetorical question. Or do you really expect an answer?" Jim leapt to his feet as the door opened.

A lighted torch was carried in, blowing their night vision.

"It's all right," a voice said in English. "I'm a friend." The light revealed a girl in her mid to late teens, with a pair of sparkling brown eyes. Her off-the-shoulder dress reached the floor. Around her neck was a gold chain, which glinted in the torchlight and an amulet on her arm. Her hair was covered by a veil, as was her face—with the exception of her eyes.

"Who are you?" Jim asked, staring at the girl.

Lou raised an eyebrow. That wouldn't have

been her first question, but she didn't think Jim was thinking straight right now. Not if the look on his face was anything to go by. Personally, she didn't trust any of these natives.

The stranger unclipped the veil that covered her face. "My name is Ailsa. I don't have time to explain. You're in great danger if you stay here. You need to leave. Now."

Lou waited for Jim to take the initiative, but it looked as if she'd have to. If only he'd look at her like that. "OK, Ailsa. How do we know that we can trust you?"

"You don't, but we don't have time to stand here and debate the issue. I promise I don't mean you any harm. If you stay here you won't see the sun rise."

"What about my dog? Is he safe?" Lou said.

"Your dog is fine. Please, you have to go now."

Jim shook Staci awake. "Come on, kiddo. Time to get out of here."

Staci stirred and gradually sat up. "OK."

Ailsa handed Jim a torn piece of paper, which was faded with age. "Here's a rough map. If you go to this place you will be safe—until morning, at least. I'll bring the dog tomorrow. Here are your things. Now please, go. Hurry, before they come to check on you."

Lou pulled herself up and took her crutches.

Staci got up and put on her rucksack.

Jim took the other bags.

Ailsa put the veil back over her face and opened the door. Having checked that the area was clear, she led them to the edge of the village, by the light of the torch. Once in the trees she looked at Jim. "Keep going. Don't stop until you reach the clearing. I'll come and find you at first light." Then she melted into the darkness and vanished.

4

Jim shone the torch on their map. "We just follow the path, I think. Over the river, down another path, take the left fork and into a clearing."

"In the dark?" Staci asked skeptically. "It's hard enough in the daylight. I'm tired."

"We all are, Stace, but the sooner we get there, the sooner you can sleep," Lou said. "And it beats being locked up in a hut that is as hot as an oven."

The three of them set off.

Ailsa's map led them down paths that were straighter than the one they'd followed the previous morning. The river was easy to cross as it wasn't too deep. After twenty minutes, they arrived at the clearing. They settled down.

Jim and Stacy were soon asleep.

Lou missed having Deefer by her side, now accustomed to him sleeping on her bed—he wasn't allowed on the beds at home. Lou dozed fitfully, her dreams full of birds and Jim statues.

Staci woke her at first light.

Jim made a fire and started breakfast.

Soon afterwards Ailsa appeared with Deefer.

He flung himself on Lou, barking madly, as if

he hadn't seen her for years.

"Get down, you silly animal. I'm pleased to see you, too." Lou made a fuss over him. "OK. I heard you. Now shut up."

Ailsa sat down beside Jim and unwound her veil. "There's trouble in the village," she began. "They went to get you at dawn."

"Annoyed to find us gone, were they?" Lou asked.

"Annoyed is the understatement of the year. They know I helped you."

"But what had we done?" Staci asked.

Ailsa took a deep breath. "The temple you slept in is sacred. They take their religion very seriously. Not only did you trespass on sacred ground, there were things missing."

"We may have moved things around a little bit, but I certainly didn't take anything."

"The punishment for violating the sanctuary is death. I tried to tell them that you were strangers so you didn't know, but they said ignorance of the law was no defense."

"How do they know you helped us escape?"

"It's a long story. The short version is I had to run away to save my life. I have nowhere to go."

"So stay with us," Jim said.

"I can't do that."

"Sure you can. Not that I exactly know where we're going, but I don't see why not." He turned to the others. "Can't she?"

Staci and Lou exchanged a long look.

"Sure, you can," Staci said

Ailsa smiled. "I don't even know your names.

29

I'm Ailsa Cudby."

"I'm James Kirk, or Jim. This is my sister, Staci, and my friend, Lou Benson. The hairy one is Deefer. Now you know who we are, and you're probably safer with us than on your own."

"Then, yes, I'd like to stay with you. Thank you."

"Mind you," Lou grinned. "You may live to regret it. We're kind of stranded here. We got shipwrecked a couple of nights ago."

"Oh, I'm sorry. Were there no other survivors?"

"Only the three of us were on the boat. Four, including Deefer. We were trying to find Jim and Staci's parents who got lost after an earthquake and tsunami, only we ended up getting lost ourselves."

"Are you from England?"

Jim grinned. "England via the Canaries, Grand Turk, and the Panama Canal, yeah."

"On your own?"

"Yeah."

"Wow, I'm impressed."

"What about you? What are you doing in a place like this?"

Ailsa's face fell. "My parents were killed in a plane crash six years ago. I was the only survivor. I was picked up by the tribe and have been here ever since."

"I'm sorry."

"Surely someone would have looked for you when you failed to arrive at wherever you were going?"

Ailsa shook her head. "I don't know if they looked for us, but no one found me. It was a small plane. Just Mum, Dad, and me. Dad was flying, the engines failed and there wasn't time to get an SOS out. He and Mum were missionaries. They'd been working on some of the other remote islands and were enroute to Pagan. We crashed here."

"Our parents are missionaries, too," Staci said. "They're in the Philippines. We're meant to be rescuing them, but we got shipwrecked here on the way there."

"Let's just hope we're not here for six years," Jim said. "We've wasted enough time getting this far."

Lou ignored the sideways glance he gave her. He could have said no and not agreed to her course changes. But she wouldn't dredge the past up now. Right this moment they had a more pressing issue. There had to be another village somewhere, hopefully one that was friendlier than the last.

"We should go," Ailsa said. "They'll be here soon. They'll search the area systematically looking for me."

The others nodded and began to pack up their few belongings. They broke camp and got to their feet.

Ailsa put dirt and leaves over the fire to disguise it. "So they won't know we were here," she said.

"I don't know about that," Lou said quietly. "Look at Deefer."

Deefer stood stiff, with hackles raised. He

looked at a fixed point in the undergrowth and was growling.

Jim followed the direction of his gaze and grabbed Staci's arm, pulling her close to him. "It's too late. They're here."

Four natives leapt from the bushes.

Lou grabbed Deefer's collar and needed all her strength to stop him from attacking.

One of the men looked at Ailsa. "So Ailsa, why you here?" he said in halting English. "These bad, broke law. You good. You like daughter. Why you help them?"

"They're from England, Amio. They don't understand your laws."

"You want go with them? Back to England?"

"Yes, I do."

Amio scowled. "Then you die with them."

The natives moved in with their spears outstretched.

Ailsa cried out in their language.

The natives stopped, glaring at her.

She spoke again and the natives backed off.

Amio looked at her. "I miss you. I no forget," he said and they disappeared back into the forest.

"Wow," said Jim. "I'm impressed. What did you say to them?"

Ailsa smiled. "Nothing they didn't already know. I assume we're not staying here."

"No. Let's move out," Jim said, picking up the bags.

Ailsa pulled off the veil off her head and shoved it in Lou's rucksack. "Am I glad to get rid of that," she said, putting the rucksack on.

"You sure you want to carry that one? It's heavy."

Ailsa smiled. "I got it. Probably easier for you this way."

Lou nodded gratefully. "Yeah, it will be. Thanks."

Ailsa ran her hands through her long, brown hair. "I don't suppose you have a hair band or pair of scissors?"

"I have a band. Actually I have loads of them" Staci pulled one from the collection on her wrist and handed it over.

"Thank you." Ailsa twisted her hair into a bun and fastened it.

They left the clearing and began walking.

Lou found it impossible to go fast as her leg hurt a lot more than usual. To take her mind off the pain she asked, "So what happened before you came to find us?"

"It was just before dawn. Amio and Mau went to the hut to give you more food. It was drugged, like the other food had been. They found me there. I'd stupidly gone back to check all your things were gone. When they found me there and you gone, they went ballistic. They told me I was no longer part of their tribe. I'd betrayed them and I would have to die instead of you. They tied me up and left me there. Outside they began the ritual drumming. They can't have shut the door properly, because the dog, Deefer, came in.

"I was trying to untie the ropes with my teeth. I guess the dog thought that was a good thing to do, because he started chewing on them, too. He bit through part of one and I was able to get an end loose. We made a run for it. If it hadn't been for him, I would be dead by now."

Jim smiled back at her. "If it hadn't been for you, we'd be dead by now and you wouldn't be in this mess," he rephrased.

"If not you, then someone, or something else. I haven't been happy there for a while. I just needed the incentive to go. Six years is a long time. I'm old enough to make my own decisions now. I want to go home."

"Seeing as how you live here," Staci said, "which way do we go?"

"I don't know. Sorry. The tribe doesn't stray far. No one ever goes more than one full day's journey from the village."

"Why?" Lou asked.

Ailsa shrugged. "Honestly, I'm not sure, but it does mean the further we go, the less likely they are to change their minds and come after us again."

They walked for two hours, Ailsa and Jim leading in front.

Staci walked with Lou.

Deefer stayed by Lou's side, apparently determined to keep her in his sight.

Staci chatted to Lou as they walked. Lou tried to listen, but found it increasingly difficult as her leg grew more painful. She lost her balance several times and finally had to ask for a rest. "Jim," she called. "I have to rest. Sorry."

Jim turned. "That's OK. I did promise we

wouldn't go too far in one go." He put the bags down. "This looks as good a place as any."

Lou lowered herself to the ground and sighed.

Deefer flopped beside her, putting his head on her lap and looking up at her.

She rubbed his ears. "Nice to sit down, huh?"

Deefer woofed and settled contentedly.

Ailsa looked over at Jim. "Jim, how much food do you have left?"

"Enough for a week, at best. Probably less. Why?"

"It won't be a problem. The forest is full of fruit, roots and things. I can find things to eat." She jumped to her feet. "Back in a sec." She disappeared off into the trees.

Jim watched her go before turning a worried gaze on Lou. "Is your leg really bad?"

"It has its moments, but right now? Yeah, it is. I don't think I can go any farther today."

"OK. We'll move on tomorrow. I can catch up with the logbook today."

Ailsa came back with her skirt full of fruit. She brushed off her skirt and sat down. "There's plenty more out there we can eat. Roots and small mammals I can cook. These are really sweet and full of juice."

As they ate, Jim still stared at Ailsa.

Lou grinned. He was besotted, which should make things interesting. They spent the next half-hour telling Ailsa about themselves.

Jim then told her about their journey.

Lou closed her eyes listening to Jim talk. The

pain was turning her stomach. Perhaps she needed to skip a meal or two here or there to avoid the nausea afterwards. Right now she would happily give her left leg for some paracetamol, although that would somewhat defeat the object of the exercise.

Jim looked at her. "Can I check your leg, mate?"

"That means moving," Lou complained.

"Only slightly. C'mon. Do it now and get it over with." He tossed her the blanket and turned his back. "See, I won't look."

Lou shook her head. "How are you going to check it without looking?"

"You know what I mean."

With some help from Staci, Lou pulled her leggings down. "This would be easier in a skirt. Maybe I should just adapt the blanket and wear that instead."

Ailsa paled. "What happened?" she asked.

"Shark, ahhhh." Lou gasped, as Jim touched her leg. Red-hot pain shot through every part of her. "Don't...please, don't touch it."

"Sorry, mate. It's not healing properly. Parts of it are infected again and I don't think the bones have set either. It's no wonder it hurts so much. You can get dressed now. It's a shame we don't have the splints I made."

"We do. They are in one of the bags," Staci said. "I picked them up just in case." She rummaged through the bag and gave them to Jim.

"Ta." He strapped them on to Lou's leg.

The relief Lou felt was immediate. "Thanks,

Jim."

"We really do need to get you to a hospital," he told her quietly.

"No chance of that," she replied just as quietly. "I'll be fine honest. I just need to rest. Pain reliever would be nice."

"Can't do that, I'm afraid. However I did bring cards. Fancy a game? We could teach Ailsa."

"Sure. Might take my mind of things for a bit."

The rest of the day passed quickly.

It didn't take Ailsa long to catch on to the game.

As darkness fell, Jim lit a fire.

Staci heated up two of the tins.

"Baked beans." Ailsa said, her joy obvious. "I haven't had these in years."

"You really have been here six years, yeah?" Staci asked.

"Since I was twelve."

Staci dished up. "That would make you eighteen then?"

"I guess so. We don't do birthdays here. It was tough at first, but I got used to it."

"When is your birthday?"

"August fifteenth."

"Five days after Jim's, then. He's eighteen, too."

After dinner, Jim, and Ailsa chatted on one side of the fire.

Staci and Lou played hangman on the other.

"I think Jim is in love," Staci whispered. "The

last time he had that look on his face was over Lara King, at school."

"Don't tease him, though. I think the feeling could be mutual."

Staci looked at her. "Do you mind? I always thought you and he would...you know..."

Lou shrugged. "No. He's made it perfectly clear he doesn't like me that way. Doesn't mean you and I can't still be friends forever though, does it?"

They settled early that night, intending to set off just before dawn in the morning to get a couple of hours in before it got too hot.

Lou woke suddenly. A weird dream lingered, not exactly frightening, but unsettling.

In the dream, a huge bird with massive wings circled above their camp before swooping ever lower. It landed and walked towards them. It looked almost like an eagle, but resembled a hawk, too, with fur in places instead of feathers. It was trying to find something. Behind it was a man, wearing tribal costume, with outstretched spear, strangely familiar.

Then Lou remembered.

Oneki.

The mythological being was part eagle, part hawk. The giver and protector of life, and the lawgiver.

The tribal man behind the bird looked like Jim.

Lou gasped as the meaning came to her.

The man was Xantic, the taker of life, the grim reaper.

And there was something else. Something important.

Lou just wished she could remember what it was.

5

At daybreak Jim was in a hurry to move on.

Lou didn't mention the dreams from the night before. She mused silently, listening to the sounds of the forest as they walked; the chattering, calling, singing and chirping of the wildlife.

They walked for three hours without a rest.

The pain in her leg grew with every step, but she gritted her teeth and carried on. Often she would stumble, the jolt sending another stab of pain through her.

The sun blazed and there wasn't a breath of a breeze.

Last night, there was something else from her dream. She couldn't remember what, but it was important to get as far away from the village as possible.

After what seemed like an eternity, Jim finally paused. "OK, we'll stop here by the river."

Lou sighed with relief and sat down. "I could really do with some painkillers," she muttered.

Ailsa overheard her and came across. "I could make you an herbal painkiller. It'll take a couple of hours."

"That'd be wonderful. Thanks," Lou said.

She shifted backwards until her back rested against a tree trunk and closed her eyes. A pillow would be nice, but right now she'd take whatever was available.

"Jim, I'll be right back." Ailsa said. "I'll find some herbs for Lou."

Lou opened her eyes, ready for the coming argument.

"Not on your own," Jim said, standing up. "Let me come with you."

Ailsa shook her head. "Jim, I've been on my own for years. We are not yet a full day's journey from the village. I know where I am and what I'm looking for. I won't be long."

"Take Deefer, then."

"The dog? Why?"

"There is no point arguing with Jim." Lou murmured. "He's a stubborn thing, at times."

Deefer sat by Lou's feet, almost asleep.

"He's tired Jim. I'll go by myself."

"But..."

Ailsa stuck her hands on her hips and held Jim's gaze. "I said, I'll go on my own. I'm a big girl now. I can take care of myself."

Lou grinned. "And Ailsa's even more stubborn than you. Fifteen-all."

Jim held up his hands. "OK, OK, I give in. You go and I'll stay here."

Ailsa disappeared into the forest.

Jim sat down.

Staci looked at him. "Jim and Ailsa sitting in a tree," she began.

Jim blushed. He picked up the logbook and

began writing.

Lou nudged her. "Don't tease him, Stace. Jim, I've remembered who two of those statues were. The bird is Oneki. He is the giver and preserver of life. He's also the lawgiver. The statue that looks like you is Xantic. He's the grim reaper, the giver of death."

"And he looks like me? Thanks a lot."

"You're welcome."

The earth moved slightly under them. "What's that?" Staci asked.

"Tremor," Jim said. "The whole area is seismically active. I imagine they get small earthquakes all the time. It's nothing to worry about."

"OK. Back in a sec," Staci jumped up and went into the trees.

Jim smiled awkwardly. "Thanks for shutting Staci up just now."

"That's OK. You really like Ailsa, don't you?"

"Yeah," Jim admitted. "Yeah, I do. I know I've only just met her, but..."

Lou tilted her head. "Love at first sight is cute. That's how Mum and Dad did it."

Jim tossed the pen at her. "I'll give you cute."

She picked up the pen and looked at it, before tossing it back. "Nope, this isn't a cute. It's a pen."

Ailsa came back carrying a whole bunch of leaves. "I'll need a pan," she said.

"Here," Jim said, handing her one. "Do you want a fire lit?"

"Please." Ailsa half-filled the pan with river water and then tore the leaves into small pieces.

She put them into the pan and then placed it on top of the fire.

Lou watched with interest. "How long do you heat it for, Ailsa?"

"About an hour or so."

Staci came back. "What's cooking?" she asked.

"Painkillers of some description," Lou told her. "Why?"

"I thought it was lunch."

"You don't want to eat again already, surely?" Ailsa said.

"That's our Staci—permanently hungry," Lou grinned. "She takes after her brother."

Jim tossed the pen at her again. "It takes one to know one. Once Ailsa has finished with the fire, kiddo, I'll do you lunch."

Staci smiled. "Thank you."

Lou tossed the pen back. "Throw that again and I'm keeping it. So is this an ointment I rub in?"

Ailsa shook her head. "No, you drink it."

Drink it? Maybe this wasn't such a good idea after all.

As soon as Ailsa took the pan off the fire, Jim opened a couple of tins and put them in the remaining pan. He whistled as he heated them.

Ailsa strained the now green liquid through a T-shirt into a bowl. She then poured the liquid into an empty water bottle. "Done," she said. "It might taste a little strange at first, but it works. You don't need much. One mouthful usually does it."

"Looks pretty." Lou took the bottle and sniffed. "Smells interesting. Tastes…" She took a mouthful and retched trying to swallow it. "It's horrid." She spluttered, and then gulped it, trying not to let the liquid touch her tongue again.

"Give it a few minutes. I think you'll find it worth it. It lasts a good six hours before it wears off. "

Jim dished up.

Staci looked at hers. "Is that all?"

"It's better than nothing, kiddo." He gave bowls to Ailsa and Lou, before continuing to speak. "The only chance we have of being rescued is to get to the other side of Agrihan. I looked at the map and chart last night. There is an abandoned air force base on the far side of the island. There might be a radio or something there we could use to call for help."

Lou snorted. "Jim. Ailsa's been here for six years. Surely she'd have found it?"

Ailsa shook her head. "First I've heard of it, but it's a big island. As I said earlier, the tribe never goes more than one day's journey from the village. All the crops are grown locally. The hunters go out in search of meat occasionally, but the women never accompany them."

"What sort of animals?" Staci asked, looking nervously over her shoulder.

"Wild boar, rabbits mainly. They set traps for them. Nasty metal ones, which they hide. We lost six villagers to them last year, but they still keep using them."

Lou suddenly realized that her leg no longer

hurt. It ached, but it didn't hurt anymore. "You were right about that green stuff, Ailsa."

"It is working?"

"Fantastic. Heaps better than pain reliever. I can't feel a thing. Does it work for migraine?"

"I don't know. I don't get headaches at all."

"Lucky you." Lou tucked the bottle into her bag. Hopefully it'd ward off any migraines she might get. She hadn't had one in a while, which wasn't a good sign. She would go weeks, and then have several cluster headaches which always left her drained.

They spent the afternoon swimming in the river, as Staci said they could wash their clothes at the same time if they wore them in the water.

Lou watched enviously from the bank as Deefer and the others splashed in the river.

Ailsa glanced over at Lou. "Want a hand into the water? You shouldn't have to miss out."

Lou looked across at Jim and then back at Ailsa. "What about my leg? If it's infected shouldn't I keep it dry?"

"There are ways around that problem." Jim mimed sawing his leg just above the knee.

Lou poked her tongue out at him. "It'd be nice if it were possible, preferably without doing that. I don't want to be a pirate..." She laughed. "Hey, I just thought, Captain Kirk could also be "Arrrr, Jim Lad" and find himself a parrot and an eye patch and then he'd be right at home on our desert island in the sun."

The others squealed with laughter.

Jim stuck his hands on his hips and looked

daggers at her.

Ailsa elbowed him. "Jim, can you give me a hand?"

Together they headed back over to Lou.

Staci took Lou's crutches.

Jim lifted her in his arms. "You weigh a ton," he joked. He waded into the river.

Ailsa held Lou's injured leg above the water.

Jim gently lowered Lou below the surface.

The water was wonderfully cool. Lou didn't want to get out.

But Jim carried her out of the water and into the sunlight to dry.

"Thank you," she said.

Jim grinned. "You're welcome. At least you won't smell now."

Lou rolled her eyes. "And I thought you were my friend."

"Oh, I am," he said seriously. "That's why I hadn't told you before." He set her down on the river bank. "Now if you don't mind, I have a sister I need to drown."

6

Lou watched the others play, her clothes steaming in the hot sunlight.

As they all climbed out of the water to join her, the ground shook again.

Jim frowned. "How often does this happen, Ailsa?"

"I've only known it to happen once before. Nothing came of it, though."

"Maybe that was your disaster, Lou," Staci said thoughtfully.

"My what?" Lou replied, puzzled.

"You know, the one that wiped out all those people."

"Oh, the pictographs in the temple? It could be. Although that said it was some kind of divine retribution. You can hardly call a volcano or earthquake that. They are an act of nature. Not an act of God. Not that I believe in God. Not like you and Jim do anyway." Lou brushed the thought off, not wanting to scare Staci, but thinking about it, the scenario fitted perfectly.

"So, Jim, where's this air force base, then?" Staci asked, changing the subject again.

Jim got out the map and showed them. "It's here. It's marked abandoned, but hopefully they left radio equipment behind."

"And if they didn't?"

"We'll cross that bridge if we get to it."

"We'll have to pass the volcano to get there," Staci said worriedly.

"That's not a problem," Jim said. He looked at Ailsa. "Is it?"

Ailsa looked at him. "The volcano is taboo. It's forbidden territory. It's the one place the natives really fear. They won't go anywhere near it. Especially with all these tremors."

"That's due to normal seismic activity— nothing worse."

"There haven't been tremors for two years. The volcano hasn't erupted since I've been here and from what I gathered from the natives, not for at least fifty years before that."

"Knowing our luck—" Staci began.

Jim cut her off sharply. "Don't say it, kiddo."

Lou looked up, the memory of her dream coming back to her, along with an overwhelming desire to get as far away from here as possible. "The other statue—the one in the temple. There were three in the inner chamber, in the place of honor. Each with their own altar. Oneki and Xantic I told you about. The other is the reason for the circular pattern to everything. The amulet and why the village is built around a central point. Jim, we have to get away from here."

"What are you talking about? Ailsa, do you know?"

"I had as little to do with their religion as possible, but she does make sense. They respected my beliefs and didn't make me go to any of the ceremonies."

Lou looked at Jim. "We have to get further away from here, from the village."

"Why?"

"Kuriarikan."

"Who?"

"Kuriarikan. The cushions and covers we used were taken from his altar."

Jim shook his head. "So....?"

"Kuriarikan is the god of fire and brimstone."

"Satan, then? The fallen angel of hell?"

"The volcano god?" Staci asked.

Ailsa nodded. "Annual sacrifices are made to appease him and keep him sweet, that sort of thing. He was personified in the volcano. If the temple was violated, a blood sacrifice had to be made or he would bring a great disaster on the village and surrounding land."

"They don't seriously think that the volcano would erupt?" Jim laughed.

Ailsa and Lou exchanged looks. "I don't know," Ailsa replied. "They haven't risked it since I've been there. There are other obscure laws concerning the volcano. Mainly about women and what they can and can't do. Being seen and not heard, for example. I may have made things worse by speaking to Amio the way I did."

Jim rolled his eyes. "Oops."

"Yeah, oops. Lou's right. We need to get further away—at least a day's journey. They won't follow us further than that."

The ground shook slightly beneath their feet.

Staci looked scared. "Jim..."

"Easy, kiddo," he said, reaching out for her. "Nothing to worry about."

"Jim, the tremors will make them come after us. We have to go now," Ailsa said.

"But it's getting dark," Staci objected.

"We can't stay here," Ailsa insisted. She covered over the remains of the fire.

Jim gathered up all their things.

"Do we follow the river?" he asked her.

Ailsa shook her head emphatically. "No, they'll expect that. Our best bet is to head for the volcano. We should be safe there."

Staci looked at Lou. "From the unfriendly natives perhaps. Don't tremors precede a volcanic eruption?"

"Not always. Only harmonic ones, not ordinary ones." She held out a hand. "Can you help me up please?"

Staci pulled Lou up and then shouldered her rucksack. "How do you tell the difference?"

"With a lot of scientific equipment. But Jim thinks we'll be all right...so lead on."

The ground shook again and Staci grabbed Jim's arm. "Are you sure that heading towards the volcano is a good idea?"

"It's the safest way, kiddo."

Staci frowned. "I don't see how, but if you insist."

Jim took Deefer's lead and they set off through the forest.

The ground shook at regular intervals.

Lou hated them because she lost her footing

with each tremor.

Staci was terrified, obvious by the way she stuck to her side.

Jim may not seem bothered, but Lou knew him well enough to know he was disturbed. He was probably praying as he walked. Not that praying would do them any good. After all, it hadn't so far.

They walked until first light.

Lou stopped. "Jim, that's enough. I'm tired. My leg hurts. Staci's exhausted. We have to stop."

Jim shook his head. "We need to keep going."

"You keep going." She leaned against the tree, slowly sliding down it. "I need to rest."

"Fine. Two hours."

"And the rest. I can't go any further. Deefer'll keep watch in his sleep if we ask him to."

Ailsa looked around. "We should be all right here."

"Too bad if we're not," Lou muttered.

"I'll take first watch," Jim said.

The girls settled down. Staci and Ailsa were soon asleep.

Deefer put his head on his paws and cocked an ear.

Jim took out the logbook and plumped down on the ground next to Lou. "Budge up a bit, mate."

Lou shifted slightly so Jim could lean against the tree, too. "How's it going?"

He opened the book and began to write. "Slowly. I decided to number the days now," he said. "I'll put the date in, followed by day whatever to indicate how long we've been on the island. For example, today is November twentieth and day three."

"Sounds good to me, but really, only day *three*? It seems so much longer than that, already. Are we really in no danger from the volcano?" she asked.

Jim glanced over at her. "We can't outrun it if we are. And at your pace we can't cover more than half a mile a day. That isn't a problem, before you say anything. I know we came looking for my parents, and I also know we're now just as lost. But there is nothing I can do about that. We just have to pray that if the volcano does blow, the blast goes the other way and not towards us."

"But we're not sharing that piece of information with Staci, I take it."

He shook his head. "That's between you and me and the logbook. And we both know she doesn't read it."

"OK." The sun blazed down and the heat and humidity rose. Lou let her eyes slide shut.

"Want some more painkiller stuff?"

"Later. I'm exhausted now. Might just check my eyelids for holes for a few minutes."

~*~

As light dawned on their fifth day on the island, they reached the edge of the lava fields. The volcano towered above them, still about a mile away.

Jim would have gone faster if he could. He

was convinced he could see a faint jet of steam issuing from the crater, but he merely left a passing note in the logbook.

He was more concerned about Lou—but he didn't write anything about that in the logbook.

What little color she'd had when they'd been shipwrecked had long since gone. She grew tired far quicker than anyone else, yet rarely seemed to sleep. And although she laughed and joked, the hollow look in her eyes was evidence that she was playing along and hiding pain. She wouldn't talk about it, no matter how much he tried to draw her out.

"We should be safe now," Ailsa said. "They won't follow us here."

Jim nodded. "OK, then. We rest here for the day."

Lou sank to the ground. "I don't feel so good," she said. The ground shook again and she half-heartedly tapped it with her fist. "I wish you would stop doing that."

As Jim made a fire, Staci and Ailsa made breakfast.

Staci looked across at Lou. "She's asleep."

"She ought to eat something though," Jim said. "I'll wake her." He shook her. "Lou?"

She groaned, but didn't wake up.

Jim felt her forehead. "She's burning up."

Ailsa went over to him. "She hasn't felt well all night, but didn't want to hold us up. The pain killer I made isn't helping anymore."

Deefer nuzzled Lou worriedly and Staci pulled him away.

Jim gently removed the splints and pulled Lou's trouser leg up. He groaned.

Red streaks ran the length of her leg and pus oozed from some of the wounds.

Ailsa frowned. "She didn't say it was this bad."

"She wouldn't. I need to clean and dress this. I'll go and get some water."

When he came back, Staci and Ailsa had changed Lou into a pair of shorts. He knelt by her side and prayed before starting to gently clean her leg. "We need to bring her temperature down."

Ailsa put a hand on his shoulder. "I'll make something to help. Can you start a fire and put some water on?"

"Sure."

Ailsa disappeared into the forest.

Jim relit the fire and heated some water.

Ailsa came back, tossed some leaves into the pan and wrapped the rest up. She put them into her rucksack. When the leaves had infused into the water, she tore her veil into strips and soaked them in it. She rubbed the cloth over Lou's face and arms and placed the wet leaves over the wounds.

Staci looked at Jim. "Now what?"

"Now we let her sleep and pray she'll pull through."

"And if she doesn't?"

"She will."

Staci shot him one of her 'don't treat me like a child' looks. "And if she doesn't?" she persisted.

Jim sighed. "I really don't know. We'll stay

put for now and see how she is when she wakes."

7

Jim sat by Lou, lost in thought, praying. Staci told him it was pointless, but he carried on nonetheless.

Over the next few hours, Lou's fever raged. Finally in the late afternoon, her fever broke. Her eyes flickered open. "Are you still there?"

Relief flooded him. "I could say the same for you. How are you feeling?"

"Better than I was."

"Why didn't you say something? Ailsa made something to help. But next time, please say something. I can't do much to heal your leg, but at least I can make sure you rest more."

Lou sat up, shifting slowly backwards to lean against the tree. "I didn't want to be a burden. The sooner we get to this air base, the sooner we can call for help, right?"

"You're not a burden. If you were, we'd've tossed you overboard weeks ago. And we've had this conversation. For better or worse we stick together. It's the only way to get through this and get home."

"Yeah." Lou tilted her head. "What about the earthquakes?"

"Nothing really noticeable since you told

them to stop. I guess they were listening."

"Funny. We should keep going. We need to find that base. See if they located your parents yet and call someone to get you guys out of here to see them or find them."

Jim frowned, tempted to call her on that, but decided against it. Now wasn't the time to pick a fight. "We will. Tomorrow."

"No, now. We've wasted enough time."

"Tomorrow." Jim gave her one of his looks. "I won't argue, but you will do as you're told for once." He lowered his voice. "Your leg is infected."

"Then the sooner we get help the better, right? And that ain't gonna happen sitting here." She scowled. "But fine, if that's what you want."

He nodded. "Yes, it is."

"Where are the others?"

"Gathering firewood and something to eat. They should be back any minute, so I'll get the fire going with what wood we have." He gave her one of his long looks and noticed her shift uncomfortably. "And I want you to eat something this time. You're losing weight again, and I don't want Staci following your example and skipping meals."

Lou half smiled. "Staci, skip a meal, what planet are you on? Staci, like you, could no more skip a meal, than Deefer could stop barking or the sun could stop shining."

"I mean it." He hardened his voice. "You need to eat to fight this infection."

She sighed heavily. "Fine. You win. I'll eat.

But just a little bit. Too much turns my stomach and then I lose the whole meal, which kind of defeats the object of the exercise."

~*~

Lou sat with her back against the tree.

Jim stoked the fire.

The cup of water next to her had been vibrating for the last hour or so, the concentric circles getting bigger and bigger. So much for the tremors having stopped—it seemed they didn't listen to her either. But then no one else did, so what difference did it make?

The ground beneath her began to move noticeably. She glanced at the others, but they didn't comment. She rubbed her leg, then stopped as that just increased the pain level. She glanced up at the volcano, blinked twice, thinking for a moment she saw smoke issuing from the crater. But the next moment it was gone, so maybe she'd imagined it. The steep slopes were silhouetted against the setting sun. It'd make a lovely photo and she reached for the waterproof bag, wincing as it was just out of reach.

Staci glanced over. "You OK?"

"Yeah, I'm fine. Could you pass me the camera, please? I want to take some shots of the volcano."

Staci reached for the bag and then staggered as the ground moved. "Great, the tremors are back."

"They have been for a while," Lou said. She

held her hand out for the camera. "At least the last hour, if not longer. But they're getting stronger again."

Staci's eyes widened. "Does that mean we're in trouble?"

"I hope not." Lou took several pictures of the volcano. "Like Jim said, we can't outrun it. Well, I can't. And I wouldn't expect you guys to stay here if she does blow her top."

Staci gasped.

Lou took her hand. "We'll be fine. Now go get your dinner, Jim's dishing up."

"OK." Staci rose and went over to the others.

Jim came over with two plates of food. "Grub's up."

Lou inhaled deeply.

Staci sat on a fallen tree with Ailsa.

Lou looked down at the plate. "Smells good." She really didn't want it, but she'd told Jim she'd eat.

Jim sat beside her. "Maybe you could help cook one day," he said.

"Maybe." She glanced at him for an instant. Was he sitting here to make sure she ate? She took a small bite, fixing her gaze on the volcano. "If you all want food poisoning."

"You ain't killed anyone with your cooking yet."

"There's a first time for everything. Besides, I've never cooked on an open fire."

Jim stretched his legs out, tucking into his meal with his usual gusto. "Nor had I. It's not that hard. Just like using a gas hob, only not so easy to turn it up or down."

Lou closed her eyes as the ground moved again. "Tremors are getting worse. I'm no expert. But I'd say they were starting to swarm. And I'm sure I saw steam or smoke at the crater."

He paused. "So have I, a couple of times now."

"Jim," she said seriously. "I want you to promise me something."

His brow furrowed. "I'm not leaving you here. So don't even suggest it."

"Listen to me. If that thing blows, and I mean *really* blows, I don't want you to wait for me. Take Staci and Ailsa and run. We both know I can't keep up on a good day, and me running anywhere for the rest of my life is out of the question. I won't have you or them die because of me and my stupid leg."

"Lou..." Exasperation tinged his voice and the scowl she loved so much crossed his face.

But he was Ailsa's now, whether either of them wanted to admit it or not. Not that he'd ever been hers, other than in her mind.

"Promise!" she said fiercely.

"OK, OK, have it your way." Jim paused for a moment as he ate. "That's *if* they want to leave you. And you know full well that they won't do that. At least, not willingly."

"Don't give them a choice." She finished what was on her plate. "It might never come to it, but I don't want anyone dying for me."

Jim glanced at her. "You realize that Jesus already did that, right? All you have to do is acc—

"

Lou shook her head. "Don't preach at me, Jim. I don't want or need it. I just need you guys to be safe, and if that means leaving me here, then that's what you do. I'll write a disclaimer in the log if it'll make you feel any better."

"Oh, really?"

She scowled back. "Yes, really."

"Something along the lines of *I, Lou Benson, being of sound mind, do hereby insist that Jim, Staci, and Ailsa leave me behind to die in the case of a natural disaster...*"

"Words to that effect, yeah." She held out a hand. "Give me the logbook, and I'll do it now."

Jim sighed, pulled the logbook from the bag and handed it to her.

Lou opened it to the current page. She chewed the top of the pen for a moment. She gave into the temptation and wrote what he'd said word for word. She looked at it for a long moment, once again chewing on the pen lid. The cup beside her moved as the earth trembled again.

Then she leaned back over the page. *I know no one agrees with my decision, but if something happens and the others need to run, I want them to do so. If need be, leave me behind. For example, if the volcano blows up, or if there is a chance of rescue—a boat or a plane that can only take three and not four. They can always come back for me later. But I do not want them staying and dying because I made a mistake and got injured.* She signed and dated it, and then gave it back to Jim. "Sign it to say you agree."

Jim shook his head. "No."

Lou growled and pulled herself to her feet. "Then what's the point of me doing that? Are you just humoring me?"

"Lou..." He reached out for her.

She shook him off. "Don't you 'Lou' me! It makes sense, Jim, you know it does." She lowered her voice. "Staci is your sister; you have to take care of her over me. She's all you have now."

"And Ailsa? I've known her a few days. You...we practically grew up together. You're like another sister."

She swallowed, bitterness filling her. "I can tell by the way you look at Ailsa that there is a whole lot more going on than either of you realize. But at the end of the day, I'm crippled and useless and you need to protect those of us who aren't. It's what the animals do, right? They abandon their injured to protect the rest of the herd. Survival of the fittest."

"We're not animals!" he snapped.

"Sometimes I think we treat them more humanely than we treat each other." She turned her back on him. "It's what I want. Please give me dignity and respect my wishes."

The birds in the trees suddenly took to the air, squawking and swirling, heading over their heads and away, in one movement.

Deefer leapt to his feet and howled.

Lou reached out and grabbed his collar. "Hey, it's all right."

Staci jumped up. "What's going on?"

The ground moved violently.

Staci staggered and lost her balance, landing in a heap at Jim's feet. He instantly wrapped his arms around her.

Lou looked at the volcano. She grabbed the camera and started snapping quickly.

A jet of red lava shot high into the sky.

The earth shook again, followed by a nonstop cascade of fiery molten rock that surged several feet upwards, before curling over and beginning to creep down the sides of the mountain.

Staci screamed, tears of fright filling her eyes. "Jim…"

"It's OK."

"No, it's not OK. We're going to die. Just like all those people did years ago. We violated the temple and now Kuriarikan wants his revenge."

Ailsa nodded. "We should go."

"And go where?" Jim looked at her. "We can't out run it."

Lou tuned them out. The lava belched high, turning the darkening sky blood red. "It really is OK. It's erupting, yes, but we're fine."

Staci turned to her, totally panicked. "You don't know that."

"Trust me. I'm doing all this stuff in geography. When it throws out molten rock like that, so long as we're not in a direct path of it, we'll be fine." Lou took some more photos. "And trust me when I say we can out walk a lava flow. Well, you guys could."

"But look how high it's going."

"Once it hits the ground it crawls along. Any volcanologist will tell you the same thing." She turned back to the volcano.

Seeing the eruption close up was incredible. News reports and clips on the Internet didn't even come close to the sounds and majesty of it.

"We have to go," Ailsa insisted.

Jim shook his head. "Lou's right. We're not in any danger, right now. And if we are I've promised I'll get you guys away."

Lou nodded. "So how about you guys go and stand over there, and pose for me? Another one for the logbook."

Reluctantly the two girls stood on either side of Jim, silhouetted against the volcano.

Lou took several pictures and then put the camera away.

Staci sat next to her, still shaking. "So how come this eruption is different?"

Lou wrapped an arm around her. "You mean if the last one killed a lot of people?"

"Yeah."

"They just are. No one knows why. Some volcanos, like the ones on Hawaii, erupt all the time, others like Mount Etna, alternate between doing this, and chucking rocks and stuff out. Some, like the Iceland ones with the unpronounceable names, just chuck up loads of ash, while others mutter and moan for a long time, and then blow their top."

"Like Mount St. Helens?"

"Technically that blew its side, but yeah. Maybe the last time this blew and caused that disaster the temple spoke about, that's what this one did. Depends on how viscous the magma is and how much gas has built up inside the volcano itself."

"Magma?" Staci asked.

"That's what they call lava before it reaches the surface."

Jim laughed. "My, my, you really do pay attention in geography."

Lou nodded. "It's my favorite subject, along with history. And I love watching disaster movies. I have so many volcano ones at home..." She broke off. "Anyway, my point is, they don't all have pyroclastic flows all the time."

Staci frowned. "What's a pyro...whatever you said?"

"A pyroclastic flow is the cloud of ash and lava that rolls down the side of the volcano really fast, like at Mount St. Helen's or Pompeii."

"Oh, right."

Lou nodded. "See when the main crater is blocked, the pressure builds up like in a kettle, or a saucepan when making popcorn. If there's a lot of gas building up inside the volcano, it mixes with the rising magma and explodes violently. The magma becomes ash and pumice and rock. But if there's no gas, then you get a lava eruption, like this one. It's just pretty and noisy, but fine."

Jim grinned. "A bit like Lou, really—the explosive and noisy type, that is. Not the pretty one. Hey, we should call this volcano Mount St. Lou."

"Personally I think Mount St. Jim would be a better name," Lou shot back quickly. "Any ash that gets thrown out causes massive problems for any aircraft flying overhead. It means they have to be diverted or grounded. All the planes in Europe were when the volcano in Iceland erupted."

"OK." Staci paused. "See this trip has turned into something educational after all." She looked over at the volcano. "It is pretty."

A while later, Lou glanced up.

Darkness had fallen completely now, apart from the sky being on fire.

"I'll take first watch if you like. Write up the log. I'll wake you at two or three, Jim."

Jim nodded. "OK, thanks."

Lou flicked through the log book as the others settled down. She didn't suppose anyone would sleep much, but then she didn't intend to either. She picked up the pen.

November 22, day 5 continued. Sometime after dark. Lou writing.

The volcano erupted. Jim was right again; just don't tell him I said so, because he's big headed enough at the best of times, without being encouraged. But so long as the lava flow keeps to the left, which it is at the moment, we should be able to avoid it. And we're far enough away for it not to be a great problem. Not that I can go very fast, but that's beside the point.

Haven't written in here for so long, I can't think of anything to say. Or a way to ruin it. Shocking, I know, but I'm out of practice. I do know a really bad beside the point joke but I'll save it for later.

It's not raining. And there's no ash fall. Which is good. Not sure I fancy camping outside in the rain. Or in an ash fall either.

I see from flicking back over several pages, that Jim said my leg's infected again. Unless we find a hospital here, and I seriously doubt we'll find one, or a large supply of antibiotics, it'll stay that way. That green stuff Ailsa made is pretty good, once you get over the really nasty taste.

My watch has stopped working. Guess the battery died. My leg hurts. Tired again, now. I sleep too much. Love the way Jim doesn't think I sleep enough. Reckon he must be sleeping on watch then, because some nights I can barely keep my eyes open long enough to lie down.

Oh, as it's later. Here's the really bad joke. I know Jim won't get it. But never mind.

Point. That's.

Lou closed the book and shifted so she was lying down, watching the eruption. Lava still flew high into the air, the ground vibrating beneath her. The force of nature, destructive, but renewing itself.

Jim would insist on it being a God thing and liken it to the human soul being renewed by fire.

She wasn't so convinced.

But that was an argument for another time.

Right now she had an erupting volcano to watch, something she wasn't ever likely to see again in her lifetime. However short that turned out to be.

8

December 5, day 18, mid-morning, I think. Lou writing.

Yes, I still have the logbook. Not sure I want to give it back, as I'm having way too much fun illustrating it. This is eruption day 13. The lava shows no signs of slowing, yet there is still no ash, which is a good sign, as we have nowhere to hide from it.

Jim wants us to stay here until the eruption stops. I did try telling him that could be weeks, but there's no arguing with him. So I spend my time sitting here, watching Ailsa make the green stuff, which incidentally, needs a far better name than 'green stuff'. I shall have to come up with one. Unless it has one. Hang on a sec, and I'll ask her.

Lou glanced up and chewed on the pen. "Ailsa, what's this green stuff called?"

"Mytona," she said looking over. "Why?"

"I figured we can't keep calling it green stuff, that's all." She turned back to the log book and wrote.

"Any chance I can have the logbook back?" Jim asked.

She grinned. "Nope, I'm writing in it."

"You sleep on it too," he complained.

"You'll live. Is that m-y-t-o-n-a?"

"Not exactly, but it'll do." Ailsa smiled. "How's the leg doing?"

"Sore. When can I have more?"

"Not until this afternoon. And only if you help make lunch."

Lou raised an eyebrow. "You want food poisoning?"

"It's fish. Not exactly rocket science."

She swallowed hard, not really liking fish, but there wasn't much choice out here in the middle of nowhere. "OK, I'll help."

"Good. You can descale them."

Lou rolled her eyes. "Oh, joy. I love doing that." She closed the logbook and slid it behind her, ignoring Jim's frown. "You can have it when I'm done and not before. Now, where are these fish?"

~*~

December 15, day 28, dawn, Jim's entry

I finally got the logbook back from Lou. Can't say I'm impressed by all the pictures that suddenly appeared but it's not worth fighting over. I did that once already and can never make up for what happened as a result.

The volcanic eruption slowed drastically last night. She's still steaming and occasionally throwing out lava, but that could continue for several weeks yet while the magma inside does whatever it does to cool down.

We stayed where we were the last few days. I wasn't going to risk setting off and getting trapped by the lava flow. But now it's time to move and start heading towards the coast again. Instead of going the way I'd originally intended, we'll head inland a bit and then swing right. Otherwise we'll hit the lava flow.

Not a good move.

And despite what Lou thinks, I'm not leaving her. I love her like a sister. And I've lost enough without losing her, too. I know we joked about naming the volcano, but it was never written down in here to make it official. So now I am doing so.

I'm sorely tempted to call the volcano Mount St. Lou. Because she can stew like that and then blow her top and vent for days —

Oy! This is Lou editing. Mount St. Jim is more like it. Or we just call it Mount Vulcan and be done with it. That deserves another shark drawn all over the next page methinks. Or better still…what's this? \ 0/

It's Jim again. I have no idea what a \ 0/ is…other than me throwing my hands in the air in sheer desperation. And no I don't get the point joke either. And I'm not going to encourage her by asking her to explain it.

Anyway, we're setting off again today. I know we can't go far, not with Lou as sick as she is. She'll deny it of course, but she's drinking more and more of the mytona painkiller that Ailsa made. So much so, that I'm now carrying it in my pack and restricting how much she has.

Having read Lou's comment about sleeping a lot, I watched her last night. Though her sleep isn't exactly restful, she's right. She falls asleep almost as soon as she lies down and doesn't stir until either I or one of the girls wake her.

Speaking of which, I need to get the fire going again and then get everyone up. It's doubtful the villagers will come after us, but I'd rather put another mile between us and them just in case. Preferably more, but I'm not too hopeful. It's been days since Lou moved more than a few feet. I fear a long walk may be beyond her.

~*~

Christmas Eve, December 24th, day 36, early morning. Jim writing.

I have begun to doubt that we will ever make the coast. Some days we barely make half a mile, other days we don't move at all. My priority has to be getting the girls safely home.

I'm trusting in God to find my parents and get them back to England in one piece. And praying He will do the same with us. What we need is a miracle, and although I'm fresh out of them, I know Someone who specializes in the miracle business.

I only have one choice left. I have to go on alone and call for help. That means finding a village in which to leave the girls, or leave them here and hope they'll be OK if the weather changes or something else happens.

During a mid-morning rest, Jim sat between Staci and Ailsa and lowered his voice, not wanting Lou to overhear him. "I was thinking, I'd better leave you guys and head for the base on my own."

"Why?"

"Lou needs help, Stace. It could be weeks before we get there at this rate."

"No. You're not leaving me."

"We stand a better chance together, Jim," Ailsa said, agreeing with Staci.

Jim sighed. "If we keep going as we are, Lou will never make it. Her leg is really bad again. She's not looking too good as it is. She's sleeping a lot more than she should do and she's losing weight."

"But then she's not eating, is she?" Staci shrugged. "So we find a village. See if they can help. They're bound to have a doctor. Or a phone."

"And how many cell phone towers have you seen around here?"

Lou hobbled over to them. "Is this a private discussion or can anyone join in?"

Ailsa smiled. "Jim wants to leave us here and head for the base on his own. We are trying to talk him out of it."

"Too right. He goes, we go. Anyway it's Christmas. Jim can't go now."

Ailsa sighed. "It's been years since I celebrated Christmas. We used to go to a midnight service on Christmas Eve. I loved singing the carols. And afterwards coming out into the still night air, where you could see your breath."

"We could sing carols later if you like. OK, it's not going to be cold, but we can still sing." Jim smiled at her.

"Thank you. I'd like that."

Lou grinned. "Where is the nearest turkey farm then?"

"No turkeys here. Just us chickens," Staci said.

Jim groaned. "Ha ha. Your jokes are worse than Lou's."

"Mine?" she scoffed. "I learned from the master as far as bad jokes go. But it isn't Christmas without a turkey dinner."

"We don't need turkey anyway. I'll organize dinner. Make it a special one." Staci added.

"You're on," Lou said. She looked at Jim. "How about we just stay put until the day after tomorrow? It's too hot to walk and two more days won't make much difference."

"We should camp by the river then," Ailsa said. "Then we'll have shade and water."

"And fish." Jim said. "Fish for dinner."

Lou felt a bolt of fear run through her as she remembered what had happened the last time Jim had wanted fish. Still, she reasoned, there shouldn't be any sharks in this river.

They packed up camp and started walking.

Twenty minutes later, they reached the river. With a clearing, trees for shade, grass to sit and sleep on and all the fresh, clean water they could drink, Jim declared it perfect. He put the bags down. "We'll stop here."

"Sounds good," Lou said. She sat down and leaned back against a tree, rubbing her knee.

Sitting around the fire that evening, the stars shone brightly in the darkness.

Deefer dozed at Lou's feet.

Staci looked across at Ailsa. "We have this nativity scene at home. On Christmas Eve we'd put all the figures in except the baby Jesus. We'd do that on Christmas morning before opening our presents. After we'd set up the nativity, Dad would tell us the Christmas story.

"There would be carols on the CD player; mince pies in the oven; satsumas and tangerines on the sideboard. Tinsel, the tree covered with lights and baubles, and cards hanging on pieces of string all over the walls. Then Mum would put the turkey in overnight—so in the morning the house would smell all Christmas-y." She paused. "Tell me a story, Jim."

Jim looked at her. "Aren't you a bit old for bedtime stories?"

"Please Jim—just this once."

"OK. What one do you want?"

"That's a silly question." Staci laughed. "The Christmas story."

"So long as you lie down. It's late."

Staci did as she was told.

They all listened as Jim told the story of that first Christmas night two thousand years ago.

Staci smiled. "Thanks Jim. We all need reminding. Usually we get so caught up and bogged down in the commercialization of it—cards, food, present shopping—that we forget what it's all about."

"A tiny baby," Ailsa said. "Who grew up to save His people."

"The best present anyone could have," Jim said. He looked at his watch. "Midnight," he said. "Merry Christmas."

"Merry Christmas," Ailsa and Lou chorused.

The night was warm and still. Ailsa looked up at the sky. "I can almost imagine the angels. Peace on Earth and goodwill to all men."

~*~

Christmas Day, day thirty-seven according to the logbook, was the hottest day since they landed on Agrihan. Hot, humid and sultry.

Even Ailsa complained it was too hot as she and Staci headed off to find enough fruit to last them the day.

Lou reckoned the temperature was well over a hundred. She was glad they weren't going anywhere today.

Deefer clambered out of the river and ran into the middle of the campsite. He shook himself vigorously, showering water everywhere.

"T'was Christmas Day and all through the camp, a wet Deefer ran making everything damp," Jim quipped.

"You get worse not better." Lou groaned, wiping her face. "That's enough, Deefer. You'll dry soon in this heat."

Ailsa and Staci came back with their arms full of fruit. "We found mushrooms to go with the fish from earlier," Staci said excitedly. "Dinner will be a feast."

"But that's not the best bit," Ailsa added. "We found a village. It's about half a mile from here."

"That's great," Jim said, a huge grin on his face. "We'll go now."

"Too hot." Ailsa shot a sideways glance at Lou. "After dinner when it's a little cooler will do fine."

She and Staci sat down and started preparing the mushrooms and other roots they had collected, while Jim started the fire.

Lou rubbed her knee. Her leg was a lot worse than she was letting on. It was beginning to smell now and she felt rotten. But the others didn't need to know that. At some point she'd confide in the logbook, in a coded entry no one else could read. Until they had to.

Jim leaned across and handed her the bottle. "Time for another dose of the mytona, mate."

"Thank you." She swallowed the mouthful and gave the bottle back to Jim. "At least I can swallow this now without wanting to throw up. We have a lot to thank Ailsa for. Not just this, but finding food and so on."

"Yeah we do." Jim looked at Ailsa and Staci across the other side of the camp.

They had their heads together and were giggling over something.

Jim glanced at Lou. "They get on well, don't they?"

"Just as well."

"What are you implying?"

Lou did her best to look innocent. "Nothing."

"Yes, you are. What?"

"Well, what with your liking Ailsa, it..." She laughed as Jim blushed. "Sorry. Seriously if we didn't get on, this trek wouldn't be much fun, would it?"

"We'd also starve."

"True. So you like her for her looks, fashion sense, or survival skills?"

"Unfair question," Jim said blushing again. "All of the above."

Lou pushed herself up. "I'll go give them a hand while you go get some more water from the stream." She slowly made her way over to the others and sat down. "Give me those fish, and I'll gut them."

Ailsa handed over her knife and the fish. "So is Jim taken?"

"Oh, please take him." Staci laughed. "No. He likes you though."

"He's very fond of you, Lou. I don't want to step on your toes here if there's something between you."

Lou snorted. "He doesn't see me as anything more than a sister or a friend. He never will."

Ailsa concentrated on the task and didn't look up. "Does he really like me?"

Staci grinned. "The word besotted springs to mind. What about you?"

Ailsa blushed and Staci giggled.

"So it is mutual then?"

"I never said that."

"You didn't have to. Your face said it for you." Lou looked at the fish. "Shame we can't make the fish purple again. That was so funny."

Ailsa looked confused. "Purple fish?"

"We dyed it to get our own back on Jim. You should have seen his face. He did eat it in the end."

Ailsa laughed. She wrapped the fish in leaves and then gave the fish to Jim to put in the fire to bake

Staci stood up. "I'm going to get some more fruit," she said. "I'll take Deefer."

"You can't go on your own, Stace," Lou objected.

"I won't be on my own. I'm taking Deefer. Anyway it's not far." She grabbed a rucksack and whistled to Deefer. "Come on. Walkies." She clipped on his lead and ran down the path, Deefer at her heels.

Lou looked at Jim.

Once Staci had gone out of sight, his face had changed. The almost forced happiness had vanished, leaving a mask of sorrow on his face.

She asked gently, "Are you OK?"

"Not really," he said honestly. "It's hard. I keep thinking about Mum and Dad and how we usually spent Christmas. The house would be decorated from top to bottom with tinsel and ceiling decorations. Dad would hang lights outside. Mum would have lit candles everywhere. I just wish I knew where they are and whether they're all right." He broke off as his voice wavered.

Lou crossed over to him and sitting next to him, put her arms around him as he finally gave in to his emotions. Lou held him as he sobbed. She looked across at Ailsa. "It had to come," she said. "He's been strong for both of them for so long now."

A few minutes later, Jim pulled away. "I'm

sorry," he said.

"For what? Being human?"

"For making such a fuss."

"Jim, real men cry. You're allowed to miss them. Grief is the price you pay for love, as someone once told me. You can't keep it locked up forever."

Ailsa sat up suddenly. She sniffed the air and looked at the others. "Can you smell something?"

The others both sniffed. Smoke drifted over the trees.

"Burning," Jim said.

Terror shot through Lou. "The forest is on fire. The lava flow must have hit something combustible and started a fire."

9

"Which way did Staci go?" Jim asked leaping to his feet.

"That way," Lou pointed.

"No. That's where the fire is," Jim groaned. "We'd better go find her." He set off into the forest calling his sister's name.

The others followed. After a bit, the smoke got thicker.

Ailsa coughed. "Jim. This is getting us nowhere fast."

"We have to find her. Staci!" Jim yelled.

Ailsa grabbed hold of him. "We need to tackle this fire, Jim. Staci has Deefer with her. She'll be fine."

Jim looked wildly at her. "Tackle this? How?"

"We have no choice. We have to."

"Other than hoping the wind changes?" Jim growled.

"And praying for rain," Lou muttered.

Ailsa rapidly improvised some fire beaters and then they proceeded into the dense smoke.

By the time they reached the actual fire, the smoke was almost like smog, the sun blotted out by the thick blackness.

Ailsa and Jim began to beat at the flames.

Lou leant on one crutch and did the best she could one handed. It was useless.

The fire was winning.

They could hear tree after tree come crashing down and being devoured by this monster that raged unheeded through the forest. They heard the animals that screamed in fear as they fled. Worse still, were the screams of pain as the fire claimed another victim. Rabbits, monkeys and the bigger predators, all fled from a common enemy, running for their lives.

Somewhere in that burning inferno was Staci.

Jim didn't know if it was that which gave them strength or the constant stream of telegram prayers. He knew the fire was gaining. If only the wind would change or it would rain, but it was for his sister that he prayed the hardest.

Suddenly Lou keeled over right in the path of the fire.

Jim pulled her to safety. He shouted over the roar of the flames to Ailsa. "How far is that village?"

"Not far. It's behind the fire line."

"Let's take Lou there. Join forces with the natives. This front will hit the river soon."

Jim picked Lou up and he and Ailsa, who carried the crutches, made their way the short distance to the village.

Behind the fire, it was a place of relative safety.

Ailsa spoke to one of the women who agreed to look after Lou, while the others fought the fire.

The woman pointed out which way to go.

Jim and Ailsa went out to join the villagers. It was exhausting, back breaking work. For well over an hour they worked without a rest. They kept at it—they had to.

Ailsa explained to Jim, using sign language, as ordinary speech was now impossible over the roar of the flames, that she needed to rest for a few minutes.

Jim nodded and Ailsa sank to the ground.

Several of the natives sat and rested too.

A tree crashed to the ground nearby.

Jim was engrossed in his work and didn't turn a hair.

Ailsa pulled his arm to get his attention. "Rest."

He shook his head.

Ailsa tugged at him. "You...must...rest...now," she insisted.

He was reluctant, but finally gave in. The smoke was thick but not choking. Jim rested uneasily. Staci was out there. Alone. Once again he was failing her. After five minutes he too got up and rejoined the others. For several hours they worked, resting for a few minutes once an hour.

The wind changed, blowing the flames east. East towards new fuel and the village. For a while no one realized, so busy were they fighting what they could see. Then above the flames came a single drum beat, loud and fast.

Jim looked questioningly at Ailsa as the natives stopped dead.

"The village," Ailsa said. "The village is

burning."

As one they headed back towards the village, all other priorities rescinded.

~*~

In the village the women frantically passed buckets of water in a chain to douse the roofs of the huts.

Lou did what she could, but it wasn't much and she sank to the ground exhausted.

Flames began to devour hut after hut, tree after tree crashing down.

The drums that someone had sounded had worked and the men came rushing back.

A small child ran across and into one of the larger huts to escape the flames.

Lou tried to alert the villagers to the danger, but she couldn't make herself understood.

Jim and Ailsa ran into the village and waved. "Jim!"

"Are you OK? You're not hurt?"

"I'm fine. There's a child in that hut," Lou pointed. "It's in the fire path. I can't move or make myself understood."

Jim nodded and dashed across the compound. As he entered the hut, flames erupted from the roof.

"Jim!" Lou screamed.

A huge tree crashed down, landing on the blazing hut.

Ailsa ran across to it. "Jim. Jim."

One of the men held her back.

She rapidly explained in their language that Jim and a small child were in there.

The two men started a rescue attempt.

Lou managed to limp across to Ailsa. What had she done? She'd sent him to his death. Staci would never forgive her. But that didn't matter because she'd never forgive herself.

Lightning flashed across the sky. Thunder echoed in response and the heavens opened. Torrential rain poured down, soaking everyone within minutes.

With the fire risk significantly diminished, all the men turned to the rescue effort. The tree was huge and had almost completely flattened the hut. Bigger than all the other huts, Lou surmised this one had belonged to the chieftain.

He and his wife stood by the girls, frantic with worry, Ailsa's translation indicating that the child was their only son.

It was over an hour before the rain stopped. The once dry clearing was now more like a mud bath, but still the rescue work went on. It was another hour after that before they had removed enough of the tree to venture into the hut. Another half-hour passed before two bodies were carried out and placed in another hut which had escaped the blaze.

Ailsa and the chieftain's wife ran over to it.

The chieftain helped Lou across.

"It's OK. They're alive," Ailsa said.

Lou's legs gave way as relief flooded her. She started to sink to the ground when strong arms folded around her.

The chieftain picked her up, carried her into the hut and set her on one of the beds.

Jim lay on one of the other beds. He was black with smoke and had a nasty cut on his cheek. He opened his eyes and tried to sit. "The little boy?"

Ailsa pushed him back down. "Alive and safe. You've got a nasty cut on your face."

"Will it scar?"

"Probably."

Lou looked at him She hid her worry and anger beneath her humor. "We all know scars are handsome, Jim and girls love them, but why did you do it?"

"That's rich coming from you. If you could have gotten there, you would have. You said as much." He sucked in a deep breath. "I couldn't leave him there. I had to do it. Then when the roof caved in, I just threw myself on top of him. I understand now why you did your hero stunt in the docks."

"That seems like a lifetime ago."

"The needs of the many outweigh the needs of the few."

"Or the one."

The chieftain and his wife came over to Jim.

The man looked at Ailsa and spoke rapidly.

She nodded and replied, then spoke in English. "He's asked me to translate for him. My wife and I wish to thank you for what you did. You saved the life of our son. We are in your debt."

Jim blushed beneath the soot and grime. "I

was just in the right place at the right time. Anyone would have done it, I just got there first."

"Do not make light of what you did. Not just anyone did it. You did. My name is Kelmac, this is my wife, Aryna. I am Chieftain of the Ashanti— the people who live in this village. We would be honored if you would stay with us for a while. You and your friends. At least until you have recovered."

"Thank you. That is very kind of you." Jim struggled to sit up. "But first, I have to go and find Staci."

"Staci? There is another of you?"

"Staci is my sister. We got separated before the fire, and she is still out there. Along with Deefer, Lou's dog."

"We will search for her. You stay here and let our doctor treat you."

"You don't understand. I let her go off on her own, I have to go and find her. He can treat me when I get back."

10

Jim groaned as he was pushed back onto the bed.

One of the natives spoke rapidly and Ailsa translated. "He says you're to go nowhere until he's checked you over."

"Not possible. I'm going to find Staci."

Ailsa touched Jim's arm. "I'll go with them and help them. We'll find her and Deefer, don't worry. We'll start at the campsite. You stop being stubborn and get checked over and then rest."

Jim shook his head and slid off the bed. "I have to find her."

Ailsa scowled. "Fine. I see the bump to your head hasn't knocked any sense into you, but I'm not letting you out of my sight the whole time." She crossed over to Lou. "Are you all right?"

Lou shrugged. "Just find Staci and Deefer."

Ailsa sighed. "I didn't think so." She spoke rapidly to one of the villagers. "Lou, this is Mafuso. He speaks a smattering of English. He's the village doctor. Nothing like you'd get back home, but better than me. Don't be an awkward patient. Let him help you. I'll look for Staci and Deefer. And I'll keep an eye on Jim, too. Keep him out of trouble."

"'K," Lou said listlessly.

~*~

Jim and Ailsa headed outside.

Five of the men were waiting for them.

Jim led them back through the now steaming and blackened forest, to the campsite they had left that morning.

The sun was setting as they reached it.

Jim's heart sank. The fire had swept through it, destroying everything it touched.

Ailsa went to the river and pulled out the waterproof bag. Unzipping it, she shot Jim a thumb's up. The contents were safe and dry.

Jim shrugged. All that mattered was his sister. "Staci." he called. "Sta-a-ci. Dee-ee-fer." No answering shout or bark came, so he turned to Ailsa, desperation flooding him. "Where did you find the fruit? It's possible she is still there or somewhere around there."

"I'll show you." Shouldering the bag, she led the way to where they had found the fruit. Here also the fire had swept through. Ailsa called again. Still there was no reply.

"I don't know where else to try," Jim said in despair.

Amilek, one of the natives, touched his shoulder. "Let's try your camp again. She'll probably head back there. We can't search in the dark anyway, and you need to rest."

"I can sleep when I've found my sister."

Ailsa shook her head. "He's right, Jim, and

chances are Staci will go back to the campsite anyway."

As the darkness deepened, they returned to the devastated camp.

Staci and Deefer sat on a rock by the river. She looked up and grinned. "Wondered where you'd all gone."

"Staci!" Jim launched himself across the clearing and threw his arms around her, hugging, laughing and crying.

Staci looked around. "Where's Lou? Why the escort?"

"Lou's fine. The escort is a long story. I'll tell you about it on the way back to the village." As they set off, Jim gave Staci the edited version of what happened.

Ailsa filled in the gaps. When she got to the part about Jim trapped in the burning building, Staci paled and stopped.

"Jim? Are you sure you're OK?"

"I am now I know you are."

Staci ran her fingers over the cut on his head, then waved her hand in front of him. "That's quite a lump. How many fingers am I holding up?"

Jim shook his head. He couldn't tell, but wasn't going to admit that to anyone.

Ailsa grimaced. "He's meant to be resting due to the bump on his head, but you know Jim. The child he rescued was the son of the chieftain. They have invited us to stay with them for a couple of days to give Lou's leg and Jim's head a chance to heal."

When they reached the village, Jim was taken to the hut that held Lou.

Ailsa took Staci to meet Kelmac and Aryna.

Deefer was tied up outside the hut. He barked loudly.

Jim gratefully sank onto the bed next to Lou and closed his eyes. "OK, you can check me over now."

Cold fingers probed and poked, but he endured it silently, figuring Lou had probably complained enough for the both of them. After a moment he forced his eyes open and looked at Lou. "Well?" he asked.

"If you mean my leg, the best word he could come up with in English was moldy."

Jim stifled a grin. "Moldy?"

"Pretty good way of describing it if you ask me." She reached a hand across the small gap and gripped his firmly. "How's the head?"

"Hurts. Your dog's barking isn't helping any."

"He's just saying thank you for finding him. Is Staci all right?"

"Not a scratch on her. I don't see how. The campsite and surrounding area was devastated by the fire."

Staci and Ailsa came into the room.

Mafuso pushed him back down. "Lie," he said firmly. "No move."

Staci grinned. "That told you, Jim." She ran over to Lou and hugged her tightly.

"Thought you were dead," Lou whispered.

"'Fraid not. Although I did wonder if you

guys were."

Lou shook her head. "Sorry to disappoint you." She glanced to the door, beyond which Deefer barked furiously. Then she looked at Mafuso. "Can't he come in, please?"

Ailsa translated and after a long pause, Mafuso nodded. "Just for a short while."

Staci went outside.

Deefer bounded in. He leapt up on the bed and covered his mistress with licks until she begged for mercy. He settled down on the edge of her bed.

"I think he wants to stay," Lou said. "He won't be any bother, I promise."

Mafuso frowned as Ailsa translated. "Jim needs to stay overnight, just to make sure his head is all right, then he will be fine. I want Lou to stay a little while longer. At least until her fever has gone."

Lou scowled. "I'd rather not."

Jim's scowl rivaled hers. "I'd rather you did. Just shut up and listen."

"Why should I when you didn't? You stormed out of here to go and look for Staci while I had to stay behind. Again."

Staci put her hands over her ears. "Oh, stop it, the both of you. I don't want either of you sick."

Lou nodded slightly.

Mafuso spoke, which Ailsa translated. "I can halt the infection, but it will return if she doesn't rest."

Jim took a deep breath. "In that case, it would

be for the best if we take Kelmac up on his offer of staying in the village. In return we could help in the rebuilding work. At least until Lou is fit."

"Fit?" Lou scoffed. "That won't ever happen, you know that."

"Fit enough to continue on to the base," Jim finished. He closed his eyes. "But I'm tired and want to sleep a bit."

Staci curled up on the bed next to him. "I'm not leaving you."

Mafuso shook his head. "You and the dog must leave."

Staci shook her head. "No." She closed her eyes, yawning.

Ailsa smiled. "She won't be in the way," she said. "And moving Deefer will do more harm than good. He'll make sure Lou stays put." She translated for Mafuso.

Mafuso finally agreed. "Just this once."

~*~

Lou pushed the food listlessly around the woven basket-like tray as the others ate and chatted over breakfast. She just wanted to sleep. The bed, really a cot, wasn't that comfortable, but it was a heap better than sleeping on the ground in the open air. Maybe she could stay here when the others left.

Jim finished the food he'd been given. "Nice not to have to cook it ourselves for once."

Staci nodded. "Yeah, it is. How's the head?"

"Still on my shoulders. Which is a good

thing." He looked at Lou. "How's the leg?"

She looked down. "Still there." She glanced up as Mafuso came over and began to remove the dressing. "What are you doing?"

"Treat leg now." He turned to Ailsa and spoke rapidly.

"OK, apparently he's got a paste made from the same leaves I made the painkiller with. If he applies it directly to the wounds, then wraps more leaves over your leg, the paste will eat the mold."

Lou rolled her eyes. "Eat the mold? Maybe he'd rather use maggots or something."

"I wouldn't suggest that," Jim commented. "Some doctors actually still do that." He got up. "Right, I'll go see the chieftain. Ailsa, can you come with me and translate?"

"Sure."

Staci looked at them. "I'll stay here with Lou." She held Lou's hand as Mafuso began working on her leg.

Lou's face creased with pain, and she squeezed Staci's fingers until they were white, but she bore it silently. She gratefully swallowed the green liquid he offered. It tasted even more bitter than the one Ailsa made, but hopefully it would have the same effect. She looked at Staci. "I might sleep a bit. Go find the others."

"Are you sure?"

"Yeah. Deefer's here anyway." She closed her eyes and opened them again. "Are you still here?"

Staci laughed. "OK, OK, I'm going." She got up. "Don't go anywhere."

"I won't."

~*~

Jim smiled at Staci as she came outside. "How is she?"

"Almost asleep. How did it go with the chieftain?"

"He's more than happy for us to stay. He said we don't have to help with the rebuilding, but I want to. These people lost a lot, and I can't expect them to just put us up when they have so little."

They sat in the sunshine on a fallen tree, eating lunch. Jim passed her some sort of bread one of the village women had given them.

The work of removing the destroyed homes had already begun.

"We missed Christmas," Staci said. "It's Boxing Day."

"I would imagine the fish is well done by now," Jim said dryly.

"Charcoal," Ailsa said.

Staci sighed. "You two deserve each other, you know that?"

Jim grinned at Ailsa. "Just because great minds think alike," he began.

"We lost everything, Jim," Staci said sadly. "Our clothes. Your logbook. My music. Lou's sewing and camera. Everything we saved from *Avon* is gone."

Ailsa beamed. "Not quite. Back in a tick." She went into the hut and returned with the waterproof bag. She gave it to Jim. "The clothes I can't manage, but everything else is here."

"Thank you." He threw his arms around her.

Ailsa blushed. "I showed you yesterday when I pulled it from the river, but I didn't think you were paying attention."

Staci hit him playfully. "Oh, stop it, Jim. You're embarrassing her. Besides your emotions are showing."

Jim immediately let go of Ailsa. "Are they?" he asked. "Sorry. I'll stop it at once."

Staci grinned at Ailsa. "Jim doesn't have emotions. It's a man-thing, apparently."

"Oh, right. I see. Good job we women have then, isn't it?"

Ailsa said nothing about seeing Jim sob when he'd thought he'd lost his sister, and for that, Jim was grateful.

"Yep. Let's go see if Lou is awake. I can feel a carol coming on. After all, it is Christmas."

11

The rebuilding work was exhausting and kept Jim, Staci and Ailsa really busy. Although Staci didn't do as much of the manual work, there was plenty of carrying and cooking to do, to keep the men fed and watered.

Ailsa was only too keen to help. "It's fun," she told Staci on numerous occasions.

"How can getting covered in mud be fun? If there were horses involved then maybe, but otherwise?"

Ailsa shook her head in mock despair. "I spent the last few years being told women were to be seen and not heard. This is a welcome relief."

"Then, go, enjoy. I'll keep Deefer out of mischief."

Jim had begun to pick up the language quickly. He'd done Spanish at school and he'd been right in originally thinking that what the natives spoke was a derivative of Spanish, with a little French throw in. And the odd English word, as well.

Despite the fact Lou's fever had abated, and Mafuso insisted she was recovered enough to do so, Lou showed no signs of wanting to get out of bed. Nor did she make any attempt to integrate herself into village life.

That worried Jim. "Maybe Lou is still ill," Jim commented over lunch. "I mean she's not arguing over staying in bed. She only ever did that when she had a migraine."

"Either that or its Mafuso's influence," Staci said.

"It's Mafuso all right, but I don't think it's his influence," Ailsa laughed. "I'm seriously considering being ill myself."

Staci laughed. "Me, too. I mean, who wouldn't want a really good looking bloke like that fussing over you all day long?"

Jim smiled. "Seriously, guys. It isn't like her not to complain."

"She's not planning on staying behind again, is she?" Staci asked worriedly.

"I don't suppose so. Why don't you and Deefer go and see how she is?"

"Sure. C'mon Deefer, let's go find Lou."

Jim waited until Staci was out of earshot before filling Ailsa in on Lou's desire to be left behind. "She was adamant that we didn't need her and there was no way she would ever go home."

"She may still not want to. In which case, we'll just have to persuade her otherwise. C'mon, lunch over. Back to work."

They had been assigned to the team involved in making a kind of mud slurry to daub over the new walls to make them waterproof.

As Jim said, "it's a dirty job, but someone has to do it."

They worked hard until dusk, with a short break midafternoon. They cleaned up in the river.

A fire had been lit and several of the women were preparing the evening meal.

While the rebuilding was going on, the meals were done communally and accommodation was cramped, but no one seemed to mind.

"It's so different here," Ailsa said to Jim. "The clothes may be the same, but the women here are respected. Honored even."

Jim looked down at his clothes.

The villagers had given them new clothes as the fire had destroyed all of theirs.

Ailsa was used to floor length dresses and Staci was enamored with hers.

Jim was yet to be convinced by his outfit. The trousers were fine, but the sleeveless tunic, worn over nothing, which didn't even fasten, left much to be desired. Not to mention very little to the imagination.

Staci offered to lend him a dress, but he refused.

He should be grateful he had anything to wear, he mused internally, not wanting Staci to know what he was thinking.

When Staci joined them she looked different

"You've changed," he said. "What have you done?"

Staci beamed at him and did a twirl. "What do you think?" Her hair, which had been almost waist length, now fell to just below her neck.

"Nice," Jim said.

"Nice?"

"OK. More than nice. Very nice. Super. Lovely. Great."

Staci shot him a filthy look, and her face fell.

Ailsa said quickly, "It's lovely. It really suits you like that."

"Thank you. Keika did it for me."

They walked across the clearing to the hut they were staying in. It belonged to Mafuso's brother, Amilek and his wife, Keika.

Keika smiled as they came in. "Hello," she said in English.

"I taught her a few English words this afty. She's been teaching me Agrihan in return." She smiled at Keika. "Shasti."

Keika beamed and nodded.

Ailsa laughed. "I could've taught you if I'd known you were interested."

"You could have taught me days ago," Jim told her. "Instead of leaving it to the rest of the natives. Fortunately, it's pretty easy to pick up." He winked at Staci. "Assuming you've already studied Spanish at school."

Before Ailsa could answer Keika gave her a bowl of fruit. Ailsa took it outside and the others followed, Keika carrying a jug.

By the fire, the rest of the villagers were gathering for the evening meal.

Kelmac said a few words and then the meal began. Meat and bread with fruit to follow.

Mafuso picked up some food and took it across to the medical hut.

"Good luck with that, mate," Jim muttered. He knew Lou wasn't eating. She was also very good at hiding it.

Ailsa looked at him. "Jim?"

"Mafuso's taken some food into Lou. She'll wait until he leaves and then give it to Deefer. Same as she always does."

~*~

Lou looked up as Mafuso came in with fruit and bread. It smelt good, but she wasn't hungry. She wasn't about to tell him that. Instead she took it and pushed the food around the plate.

"Eat," Mafuso told her.

Lou shook her head. "I'm not hungry."

"Eat or I will feed you."

As tempting as the thought was, Lou decided to do as she was told.

Mafuso watched her eat a bit and then went out to join the others.

Lou immediately let Deefer eat the rest of the food, except one fruit.

When Mafuso returned she was nibbling on the fruit.

"I stay here tonight," he said in English.

"I don't need a bodyguard," Lou said, making the meaning of her words obvious.

"Are you being awkward?" Jim asked.

Lou jumped, not having heard or seen him come in. She glared at him. "I don't need a bodyguard. I can take care of myself."

"You'll do as they tell you. Did Deefer enjoy the dinner again tonight?" Jim asked and sat on the edge of the bed. "You have to eat, Lou."

Lou turned her face away.

Jim sighed. "If you don't eat, you won't recover."

"So?"

"We can't stay here forever."

"Well, you go then. Deefer and I will be fine on our own."

"Don't start that again," Jim said crossly. "Think about someone else for a change. Staci misses you."

"She's got Ailsa. So have you."

Jim looked at the ceiling. "For crying out loud, Lou. Is that it? Are you jealous?"

"I am not." She turned and looked at him.

"Yes, you are. Listen, Ailsa will never replace you. She doesn't have your twisted sense of humor, for a start. You are my best friend in the whole world—more like a sister, actually. I love you. I need you. I will never leave you here."

"You may have no choice." Lou winced as Jim's arm brushed against her leg.

"That hurt?" he demanded. "I barely touched you. Show me."

"No."

Jim grabbed the hem and pulled Lou's skirt up to expose her leg. He groaned and shook his head. "How could you let it get that bad? Let me get Ailsa and she can translate for us. I've picked up a fair chunk of the language, but she's way better than I am." Jim quickly returned with Ailsa.

"Mafuso says you are not a good patient and won't let him treat you," Ailsa translated.

"It hurts," Lou replied sullenly.

"It'll hurt more if it is not treated. The infection will grow and you will die." Ailsa carried on translating. "Mafuso says he can only do so much. You have to want to get well otherwise there is no point in being here."

Jim raised his voice. "You will never be able to take Deefer for a proper walk again. Is that what you want? Never to run or climb or dance or throw yourself off rope swings? If you won't do it for us, do it for Deefer. He doesn't understand at all. He wants his mistress back. He likes us, but no one can replace you. He's a one woman dog, Lou."

If she would stay without them Lou would need Deefer and she would need to be well. She also needed to buck her ideas up so they wouldn't guess what she was planning. Besides, Mafuso was one good-looking man and maybe...just maybe if she was good, he'd feel the same way about her and let her stay with him when the others left.

She looked across at the tall, dark haired native and nodded. "OK, Mafuso. I won't argue anymore."

Ailsa translated and Mafuso smiled. Ailsa translated his reply. "He wants you to teach him a bit more English." She laughed. "So that he can argue properly with you."

"Only if he teaches me his language in return. So that I can argue back."

Mafuso nodded.

Jim gave an audible sigh of obvious relief.

That night Lou didn't sleep.

Instead she and Mafuso taught each other words and phrases, starting with parts of the body and then other things in the room.

When she finally fell asleep as the sun rose, not only had she learned a lot, she had fallen heavily for her new friend.

12

January 3rd, day 46. Way too early as it's still dark. Jim writing.

The rebuilding work is finally completed and the forest, amazingly, has begun to recover from the devastating fire already. And the volcano, which is really called Agrihan—apparently the whole island is the volcano—has quieted down and ceased all activity.

Lou is living with us now and we're still with Amilek and his family.

Mafuso said at least this way he could keep an eye on her.

She spends most of the day with him and is semi-fluent in Agrihan now. As he is semi-fluent in English, they get on really well. Suddenly she'll do whatever he says without complaining. Which is a grave cause for concern. Their growing friendship, that is, not the fact Lou is eating and getting better now. If she gets too attached to him, she will want to leave less than ever. And Staci won't leave without Lou. Staying here forever simply isn't an option.

Now Lou is recovered sufficiently to move around again, I want to leave as soon as we can and head for the base. It's not that I'm ungrateful or anything, but I need to know what happened to Mum and Dad, and Nichola deserves to know we're all right. If she won't have us back…if Mum and Dad didn't make it…then we need to find somewhere to live in England on our own. Staci needs to go back to school.

Or maybe Nichola could look after Staci, and I'll find a place…maybe with Ailsa, if she'll have me.

Anyway, the men are going hunting today, and I'm taking the opportunity to go out with Amilek and Mafuso, hoping to get a chance to talk to him. Ask what his intentions are. Lou doesn't have a brother to protect her and look out for her. She only has me.

Jim bided his time as they set off shortly after dawn, and made small talk for the first part of the journey. When they were an hour from the village he stopped.

Mafuso turned to him. "Do you need to rest?"

"For a bit. Can we talk?"

"Sure."

They sat on a fallen tree. Jim having started the conversation, paused, unsure how to continue. He opened his mouth, decided that wouldn't sound right and closed it again.

Mafuso smiled at him. "I can guess what you want to talk about."

"You can?"

"Yes. You want to talk about Lou. My intentions towards her," he said carefully.

Jim grimaced. "You took the words right out of my mouth. You make me sound like her brother. I'm not. I just feel kind of responsible for her as she doesn't have anyone else. Do you have feelings for her?"

"I have feelings for her, yes. But not love. I

am, how you say, to be joined to someone else."

"Engaged to be married."

"That's right. To Tayba. She is to be my wife in five days. I will take you to meet her. She will bear me many sons." Mafuso stood up. "We must carry on. Kelmac is expecting us back with meat before sundown."

Jim stood up, relieved that there was no possibility of anything more than friendship between Lou and Mafuso, but unsure of how she would take it. They checked the next trap. A rabbit lay in it.

Mafuso put it in the sack and reset the trap.

Jim asked, "How long have you been engaged?"

"Not long. Kelmac will make the announcement tonight at dinner."

Jim grasped his arm. "Will you tell Lou before then? It would be better coming from you."

"I will do it when we get back." Mafuso replied. "No problem."

Jim grinned at the phrase. Mafuso had learned fast.

They carried on checking the traps and emptying them.

Mafuso showed Jim how to open the trap, free the dead or dying animal and reset it.

Jim looked closely at the jagged teeth. "It's rusty. Don't you ever clean or replace them?"

"There is no need. The rain cleans them and the heat dries them."

"They're lethal."

"That is the point of them."

Jim looked up as a sudden thought hit him. "But what if, I mean, what if a child or..."

"People get caught in them? It happens. It is best to stay on the path. I have explained this to Lou. She needs to be careful with the dog." Mafuso stood up. "We have made good time. That's the last of them."

"Shall we head back?"

"Yes."

Mafuso hoisted the bag over his shoulder and was about to set off when a squealing noise and a thudding of feet came through the brush.

A wild boar charged through the trees, its eyes glinting, its head down and tusks lowered. It was headed directly towards Jim.

A bolt of fear shot through him.

Mafuso ran past him, a spear flexed in his hand. He thrust hard above the pig's shoulder, stabbing deep. Mafuso's arms rippled as he stood his ground, holding the spear in place, his leg muscles corded as he used every ounce of strength he possessed to keep the spear in the pig.

Enraged, the beast tried to turn, damaging itself further as it fought. And then, just like that, it was over. The boar took a reflex step, and then fell to the ground.

Mafuso waited a moment, keeping his distance while checking the boar out. He approached, put a foot on the hide and pulled to retrieve his spear. He turned to Jim. "Are you all right?"

"Fine," a shaken Jim replied. "Thanks you."

"You're welcome. We shall feast tonight." Mafuso approached the hog, slit it open and began to expertly field dress the meat.

Jim watched in fascination, having never seen the operation.

Once Mafuso finished, he cut a pole from one of the trees, tied the boar's feet together with vines and slipped them over the pole.

Jim knew what to do from photos he'd seen in his world history class. Jim took one end of the pole, Mafuso grabbed the other and they carried the boar back to the village.

On their arrival a huge crowd surrounded them. Kelmac and Aryna made their way through to greet them. He congratulated them on the boar.

"It was all Mafuso's doing," Jim explained. "It charged at us. I froze. He killed it with his spear."

Kelmac looked at Mafuso. "Is this true?"

Mafuso nodded.

"You are indeed a great warrior. Tonight we feast in your honor. Lifesaver and warrior."

Some of the others bore Mafuso on their shoulders around the village.

Staci and Ailsa, as always had run to Jim's side.

Lou stood on her own outside the hut. She turned and headed slowly down the path, Deefer trotting by her side.

Jim started to follow her.

Staci tugged his arm.

"What is it?" he asked.

"You should go wash. There will be an

announcement of some kind tonight."

"But Lou?"

"She's been in a weird mood since lunch. She'll get over it." She hugged him tightly. "My brother, the hero."

Jim shook his head. "No, I'm not."

"OK, you're not. Either way, you stink. So go wash."

~*~

Lou sat on her own by the river, Deefer by her side. Thoughts cascaded through her mind, the wind blew in the trees and some kind of insects chirped in the underbrush.

Footsteps suddenly echoed and Mafuso sat beside her. "Hi."

"I wondered where you were. You were not there when we returned from the hunt."

"I was there, then I came here to think. I hear you saved Jim's life."

"He is my friend. As are you."

"Good. You're my friend, too."

Mafuso laid a hand on hers for a moment. "I have to speak to you. About something important."

Lou tugged her hand away. She took a deep breath, burying how she felt. After all, she'd become expert at that recently. "It's OK, Mafuso. I know what you plan to say."

"You do?"

"Tayba's a nice girl. She loves you. We were on kitchen duty together all day. She talked about you and the wedding nonstop. I hope you'll both be really happy together."

"Thank you."

"You're welcome." Lou changed the subject. "C'mon. Let's go have some of this pig you killed."

Together they found Tayba, and Mafuso introduced her to the others.

Jim congratulated them. Then he turned to Lou. "She is beautiful, but not a patch on Ailsa," he whispered.

Lou shook her head. "You got it bad, mate. You've known her a few weeks. You can't make a life decision based on that."

"Try stopping him," Staci laughed. "C'mon, I'm hungry."

They queued up for food and then all sat together.

Amilek and Keika joined them.

The conversation soon turned to the weather.

Amilek looked at the sky. "It will rain soon."

"How can you tell," Lou asked as she picked at the meat. "Not a single cloud anywhere."

"It's summer," Amilek explained. "In summer it rains. Much rain."

"In England it always rains."

Jim corrected Lou. "Not all the time. We have three types of weather. It's either raining, about to rain, or just finished raining."

"And in the summer, we have warm rain." Staci added.

"You are blessed it rains so much," Mafuso said as he appeared from nowhere. He was good at the silent approach. He seemed to know when she wasn't eating and would show up, giving her no choice in the matter. He sat, Tayba at his side. "Some years the rains do not come."

"Then what happens?" Staci asked.

"Crops fail, animals die. Things are hard when the rains do not come. This year they will come. I can smell them."

Staci sniffed. "Can't smell anything except dinner."

The others laughed.

"You will see. The rains will come in the morning." Mafuso looked over at Lou. "Is your meal all right?"

Lou had barely touched it. "It's fine."

"Good. Then eat."

She picked up the meat and took a bite. It threatened to choke her, but somehow she plastered a smile on her face and joined in, despite the fact her heart was breaking.

Kelmac stood and raised his hands.

At once everyone fell silent.

Ailsa quietly translated.

"Tonight we feast in the honor of Mafuso, whose heroic deeds brought us the food of the elders. We celebrate him and give him great praise for his deeds."

A cheer went up.

Kelmac continued. "We also announce his joining to Tayba, daughter of Lotho and Sivelle. The ceremony will be in five days."

Another cheer went up.

Tayba blushed and hid behind Mafuso. As

normal conversation resumed, she said, "You will be staying for the wedding?"

Jim glanced at Lou. "We really ought to be heading off now Lou's better. We can't stay here forever."

"Five days won't hurt," Ailsa said. "It would be nice to stay for the wedding. Please?"

"Lou?"

"You know my feelings on going home, Jim. Besides, it's rude to refuse an invite from the bride. We'd love to stay. Thank you."

"I guess that's settled, then. Thank you."

The next morning was wet. They awoke to the steady drumming of rain on the roof.

Staci looked outside. "Stair rods," she pronounced.

"What are stair rods?" Keika asked.

"Bannisters that go up a flight of stairs," Jim tried to explain, not very successfully.

So Lou tried instead. "Cats and dogs," she said helpfully. "Torrents. Chucking it down. Couldn't be wetter if it tried. Lovely weather for ducks."

Keika looked outside. "Ah, much rain."

13

January 6th, midday-ish, day 49, Lou scribbling.

I'm a fool. But you knew that, right? I give my heart in the most stupid places. I mean, I'm just a stupid kid. Why would he want me? Why would either of them...or anyone come to that...want me? And if you notice I'm writing this backwards, that's because Jim can't read mirror writing. At least, not without the aid of a mirror. And there isn't one here.

Which means for now, at least, I can pour out my heart and no one will know. Because I have no one to talk to. I'm alone in a crowd of people, and I always will be. Anyway, the wedding is two days away and Jim is planning on leaving as soon as it's over. Not that he's put as much in here, but I know him and the way he keeps looking at the others when everyone's sleeping. He wants Staci home and safe. And so do I...but I'm not going.

Once we find this base, I'll write a proper explanation, but for now, that stays between me, myself, and I. OK, back to normal writing now, else Jim will complain too much.

And yes, it's still raining. Life doesn't stop though. The hunting and gathering continues as normal, along with the construction of the new home for Mafuso and Tayba. The women meet daily in

*Kelmac's home, making wedding garments for Tayba.
Each day as the rains fall, the house grows bigger and
the wedding dress nears completion.*

*Jim's addition. Will deal with Lou and her
illegible entries later on.*

*I sought out Kelmac an hour or so ago. He was
sitting in the small chapel they have here. I assume a
missionary built it at some point in the past, which is
probably where some of them learnt their English from.*

"Kelmac?"

The chieftain turned and smiled. "Hello,
Jim."

"I was wondering if I may speak with you."

"Of course. Please, sit."

Jim sat beside him. "We have been here some
time. Not that we don't like being with you all,
but we should leave. Try and get to the American
base and send a message home."

"I have been there once, many years ago.
There is no one there now."

"I was hoping to find a radio. So someone
can come and get us."

"If there is not, you may return here. You are
always welcome to make your home here."

"Thank you. I shall remember that." Jim
bowed and took his leave. He hoped that
wouldn't be necessary.

Lou had closed herself off completely. She
wasn't eating, and wasn't letting Mafuso treat her
leg anymore. When Jim had tried talking to her,
she was the proverbial brick wall and just blanked
him. About the only thing he could do was pray.

Pray they'd find the base.

Pray that there was a radio there and they could call for help.

And pray that help would come before it was too late.

~*~

Lou tried to explain the concept of honeymoons to Tayba, Aryna, and Keika as they prepared the midday meal. Marriage was taken very seriously here. One woman bound to one man for life—no exceptions. Literally until death do them part. Like the relationship her parents had had, right up until her father had been killed. Then one was just alone.

Like she was and always would be. But that didn't mean that Tayba should miss out on what normally happened. At least in the western world.

"It's a two week holiday immediately after the reception, uh wedding feast. The groom keeps the destination a secret from the bride, but it's usually somewhere exotic."

"Exotic?" Tayba asked.

Lou grinned. "Hot and sunny and not in England. It's their chance to be alone and get to know each other properly without the distraction of work and friends and family. But before that and the wedding, there's the hen night."

"The what?"

"The hen night. It's a party for the bride and her female friends before the wedding. The groom and his male friends have one on the same night. That's called a stag night."

Aryna looked up from her work. "What happens?"

"It's just a party. All the women bring presents for the bride, usually little things for the house. Or chocolate. Then they eat, drink, and play silly games. The men usually get drunk and tie the groom to a lamp post fifty miles from home."

They didn't understand that, so she had to explain more.

Shocked silence met her.

"It doesn't happen very often though. It's just a last fling with your mates before you commit yourself to someone for life."

"It sounds lovely," Keika said. "When does it usually happen?"

"Traditionally it's the night before the wedding, but most people have it a few days before."

Tayba looked at Aryna. "Please speak to Kelmac. We do not have much time. Perhaps tonight?"

"I will speak with him now." She went in search of her husband. She was gone only a few minutes before retuning. "He agrees. We may have them tonight."

Plans swiftly got underway.

Lou and Jim, being the token British man, found themselves expected to organize the parties.

It didn't take long before an irate Jim sought her out. "I don't know what to do," Jim grumbled. "I've never been to one. Trust you to come up with the idea."

"We were just talking. And I haven't been to one either." Lou scowled. Why was this her fault? "The important thing is they enjoy it."

"Can't we do a joint one?"

"No. You come up with your own ideas."

Jim glared at her. "But it wasn't my idea, was it? It was yours. And I've got three hours to plan and get my work done at the same time."

"Jim, it's the least we can do for them. They have fed and clothed and housed us. What little they had left after the fire, they willingly shared with us. Besides if you are leaving after the wedding, it's a good a way as any to say goodbye."

"Aren't you coming with us?"

"Yeah, of course I am," Lou answered quickly. "The others might not want to leave, though."

Jim scowled. "You know very well the only stumbling block to going home is you."

"Yeah, well, I have an appointment with Mafuso and a party to plan. You go plan yours and worry about going home in a couple of days' time." She swung away on the crutches, whistling to Deefer.

~*~

It was worrisome to Jim that she continued to use the crutches, despite Mafuso's best efforts to convince her that she no longer needed them. Her leg seemed to hurt continuously, although she told him constantly it was fine, and that it didn't bother her anymore. Yet she remained on the crutches.

Mafuso had checked her over. "It does not hurt? Your wounds are healing."

She shook her head. "You did a good job. Thank you. I'll miss not seeing you every day. You said yourself it's healed, so I needn't waste your time."

He frowned, and then took her hand. "You are not wasting my time. Neither do you need the crutches to walk, you know that very well."

"There is no way I can keep up with the others without them," she insisted. "Or Deefer. And I can't stop taking him for walks and stuff. Even if it is just around the village."

"But on those..." Mafuso paused. "You are a pretty girl, but how will you find a husband if you can't..." He broke off.

She pushed to her feet. "I know you mean well, but I'm fine like this, honestly. It's not like I'm ever planning to get married or anything. And speaking of weddings, I have to go plan this party for tonight. See you later."

She headed outside and over to join the others.

Jim had no idea what to do for Lou at this point. And he had a stag party to plan before he could think how to solve any other problems.

~*~

Lou could hear Staci complaining from half way across the clearing. She stopped just short of the group to watch.

Keika had explained that the fabric had come from the missionaries, and more from when the air base was still occupied on the island. The tribe hoarded it, despite occasional ships that stopped in their little bay and brought modern goods.

Staci moaned loudly about the sewing in her hand. "This is more Lou's thing than mine. I don't know one end of a needle from the other."

"Which is probably why you're here," Ailsa told her. "It's about time you learned."

Staci grumbled and managed to prick herself more than the fabric. Her stitches were large and uneven and she even managed to sew the fabric to her own dress. This may have been amusing or an accident, but her comments had been loud and long and this seemed another excuse to get out of it.

Ailsa unpicked the stitches and freed the fabric from Staci's skirt.

"Can I go now?" Staci said.

"No," Keika told her. She took the fabric from Ailsa and gave it back to Staci. "You must learn and do your share of the work. Here, I will help you."

Lou grinned.

As far as Staci was concerned, 'help' usually meant someone else doing the tasks she didn't know how to do. She felt incapable of learning some things, and often confided to Lou that she hated disappointing people when she failed. The girl was in for a shock.

Keika showed her how to hold the fabric and needle correctly and how to do four tiny precise stitches. She then gave the fabric back to Staci. "You do it now."

"But I thought...." Staci mumbled.

"I have my own to do. I will help if you get stuck. We have to work together here, or we do not survive."

"If I must." Staci stabbed the fabric with the needle and with considerable effort, managed to make her stitches smaller and more neat.

Finally the horn to signal stopping work sounded.

Staci sighed thankfully.

Jim came across on his way to the river to bathe. "Did you have a good day?"

"No. They put me on sewing. I hate sewing."

Ailsa laughed. "What she means is she couldn't sew if her life depended on it."

Staci glared at her, then grinned sheepishly and took off towards the hut they were staying in.

Jim made to go after her, but Ailsa stopped him. "Leave her. She's been complaining all day, but she did do the task, even though she didn't like it much."

Lou turned away, not wanting to see another moment of closeness between someone she liked and the person they preferred over her. She headed after Staci. "Stace, wait up."

Staci turned. "I hate sewing. I've done nothing but sewing for days—I know I've been complaining, but I don't do it very well and I don't like doing something I'm not good at."

"Well, if you don't like it," Lou interrupted, "then do something about it."

"Like what? Jim keeps saying how we owe these people and need to do what we can to help."

"You could tell him you want go home. He wants to head on to this base, try to radio back home for help. He's only staying out of a sense of duty, but his first duty is to you."

"But going home would mean going to boarding school if they haven't found Mum and Dad."

"At least you wouldn't have to sew all day long. You could see your friends, have someone else take care of you instead of having to do it all yourself. And my mum would have you for the holidays."

"Jim takes care of me now."

Lou sighed in exasperation. "Stace, Jim is only eighteen. He doesn't need this huge burden of responsibility. He feels totally responsible for stranding us here, even though it isn't all his fault. Besides, Jim wanted to join the military. He can't do that from here or if he's caring for you on a full time basis. Can he?"

"No, he can't." Staci took a deep breath. "OK. Home, it is."

"Are you sure it's what you really want?"

"Yeah. To be honest the novelty wore off a long time ago. I just never had the courage to say so. I kept going because of him."

Lou shook her head. "So you were doing it

for him, and he was doing it for you?"

"Yeah. It's that downward spiral of consequences again, isn't it?"

"Yeah, something like that."

Ailsa came over to them. "We must get ready for the party," she said. She looked from one to the other. "What's going on?"

"I want to go home," Staci said. "I have for ages. Today just made up my mind for me."

"Have you told Jim yet?"

"No. I'll tell him tomorrow. I want to stay for the wedding. What will you do?"

"I don't know." Ailsa paused as Staci's face fell. "Of course, I'm coming. I want to go home, too. I have no idea what I'll do when I get there, but hopefully something will turn up."

"Maybe Nichola will help," Staci said. "Or, if they've found Mum and Dad, you could come live with us. Jim would like that." She grinned. "Unless he's already proposed."

Ailsa blushed and tugged Staci's hair. "I wouldn't tell you even if he had."

"I'm his sister. You have to tell me everything. Actually, when he does propose that will make you my sister and then you won't have an excuse to keep secrets from me."

Lou turned away, heading slowly across the clearing. Now more than ever, she was the outsider. The sooner the next few days were over, the better.

14

Lou sat quietly in the hut, rubbing her leg absently.

Keika came in and smiled at her. She unfastened her hair and began to rebraid it. "Are you all right?"

Lou took a deep breath. "If I decided not to go with the others, would I be able to stay here?"

"Here? With us?"

"In the village, somewhere; not necessarily here with you. I don't want to impose. I could sew, help cook. I'd pay my way."

Keika studied her for a long moment. "It would be Kelmac's decision."

"But would you speak for me?" She paused, switching to Agrihan. "I mean, if I ask, would you second my application to stay."

"Why don't you want to go home?"

"I have nothing to go home for," she said quietly. "All that matters is that the others are safe. Once they are, and if I can come and live here, things will be fine."

Keika held her gaze and nodded. "I will speak with him once you have," she said.

"Thank you. I'll find him tomorrow and talk to him then."

"You will need to phrase your request in such a way, that it doesn't look as if you're abandoning your friends."

"I'm not. It's just better this way." Then as the door opened and the others came in, she switched back to English. "Is everything ready, Stace?"

Staci nodded. "Yes, it is. All the food is ready and divided between the two groups, bar that last tray which is to come with us. Jim will keep the men over on the other side of the village."

Keika smiled. "That's good. I hope things go well tonight, for everyone."

Staci nodded. "I hope so, too. Otherwise Lou will never be asked to throw a party again. Anywhere."

Lou pulled herself to her feet, leaning heavily on the crutches. "I won't be either way. Come on. Let's go. Can someone bring the bag?"

"Sure." Ailsa grabbed it. "What's in here?"

"Couple of bits I need. Nothing that exciting."

Keika picked up the last tray of fruit and led the way outside.

Ailsa crossed back to the others and she and Staci followed.

Lou swung herself slowly behind them. She took a deep breath. If this didn't work, they wouldn't let her stay. She had to make a good impression tonight.

Outside all the women began to gather under the huge woven leaf awning the men had fixed up for them.

Tayba looked nervous, but then she had no idea what to expect.

Lou crossed over to them and they all sat down. "The whole point of the next few hours is to have fun," she said. "Not to make fun of Tayba or embarrass her." She opened the bag. "Where we live, tradition states that the bride has to wear a veil." She pulled out a cream length of fabric which Keika had found. She carefully fastened the veil in Tayba's hair. "Just so we don't forget who the bride is."

Her voice was drowned out by laughter. For a moment she wasn't sure if it was her Agrihan or if they'd genuinely found what she said funny.

Hoping it was the latter, Lou continued. "Now I'm handing over to Aryna for a moment. She has something important to do."

Aryna took the bag from Lou and gave it to Tayba. "These are for you, from all of us."

"For me?" Tayba asked.

"Yes. Giving the bride gifts is a custom we all share."

"But everyone lost so much in the fire, it hardly seems fair that…"

Keika hushed her. "That does not mean you have to start with nothing. You will become the wife of our healer, second only in standing in our community to Aryna, but more importantly, you become my sister."

For the next twenty minutes, Tayba pulled her gifts one by one from the bag. A pile of coconut shell cups, woven trays, and some of the precious cloth grew next to her.

She was moved to tears by the love and generosity her friends and neighbors had shown her. She spent ages looking at each gift as she opened it.

She pulled the last one from the bag and unrolled the fabric gently. Her eyes widened at the cross-stich picture of the sun rising over the beach. She looked at Lou.

"It's from us," Lou said. She'd worked hard at finishing it in what little time she had. She hadn't wanted to give the white horses on the beach away—that one was in her bag with instructions to give it to her mother. She'd started the sunrise picture just before the hurricane. "It's cross-stich. I made it."

Tayba looked back at the fabric. "You made this?" She asked.

Lou nodded.

Tayba hugged her tightly. "Thank you. I will get Mafuso to make a frame for it."

All the other women gathered around to admire the picture.

Next they ate. Raucous laughter echoed across the village.

"The men sound like they are having fun," Ailsa said. "Maybe we should go see what they are up to."

Staci shook her head. "No way. Once we've eaten, we'll be the ones laughing."

"Why? What have you got planned?"

"No idea." She looked at Lou. "Bet it'll be fun though."

Lou glanced up from the piece of fruit which

she'd hardly touched. "I thought we could play the sad and solemn occasion game."

"Never played it."

"It's easy."

"Really?"

Lou nodded. "Yeah, really. I'll explain it in a bit."

Once everyone finished eating, she began to explain. "Everyone sits in a circle. You then turn to the person on your left, look them straight in the eyes and say, 'this is a sad and solemn occasion,' without smiling, laughing or breaking eye contact. But you can say it in whatever tone of voice you like."

"That's it?" Keiko asked.

Lou nodded. She turned to Staci. "This is a sad and solemn occasion."

Staci raised an eyebrow. "Piece of cake." She turned to Keiko. "This is a sad and solemn occasion."

Easy to begin with, it became increasingly difficult as the game progressed.

Staci broke eye contact with Lou, making her have to repeat herself. Then Staci cracked up laughing and caused a ripple of laughter which spread and grew, until eventually no one could keep a straight face.

Then they moved onto some of the other just as silly games that Lou had planned. By the end of the evening, they had all laughed until they'd cried.

As she left to go home Tayba gave Lou a hug. "Thank you so much. For everything."

"You're welcome. It's been fun." The girls made their way back to the house.

"The men have gone very quiet," Staci said. "They obviously can't take the pace."

Ailsa yawned. "Nor can I," she said. "I hadn't realized how late it was. It must be about midnight."

"How can you tell that?"

"Position of the moon. Easy when you know how."

They crept into the hut, but the men weren't there.

The girls lay down and were soon asleep.

Lou lay there with a hand on Deefer's collar. She'd just dozed off as dawn's early light broke over the village, when someone tripped over her crutches and landed heavily on her leg.

"Sorry," Jim said. "Did I hurt you?"

"It's fine. What time is it?" she asked, holding her leg, somehow keeping in the groan of pain.

"Dawn. Go back to sleep. We have to be up in about three hours."

"You get the DSO," she yawned.

"DSO?"

"Dirty Stop Out award."

Jim grinned, and lying down was asleep before his head hit the pillow.

Lou watched him for a while before closing her eyes.

Mafuso and Amilek come in, but rather than sleep, they sat by the fire talking quietly together.

She didn't want to listen, but the voices carried. Tears burned her eyes, as Mafuso confirmed what she already knew, but she wouldn't let them fall. There was plenty of time for that later.

~*~

Surprisingly all the men, except Jim, were up by seven and ready to do a day's work. He moaned as Lou shook him.

Lou pulled the covers off. "Get up." she said unsympathetically. "You only have yourself to blame. Now get up or I set the dog on you."

He didn't move.

Lou sighed. "Deefer, lick him."

Deefer immediately started licking Jim's face until he reluctantly got up.

"OK I'm up. I shall go and throw myself into the cold river to wake properly."

"Mind the shark doesn't get you."

He raised an eyebrow. "Shark. Yeah, right. Since when have you seen a shark in the river?"

Lou rolled her eyes. "You should have paid attention in your geography lessons. Look out for the piranhas as well."

The day was spent decorating the village and making the final preparations for the wedding.

Jim spent most of the day dozing under a tree, and Lou wisely left him to it. He'd only be crabby and bad tempered if she disturbed him again.

Mafuso found her as she crossed the clearing. "The picture you gave us is beautiful. Tayba made me make a frame for it this morning. It will take pride of place on the wall of our new home. Thank you."

Lou smiled. "You're welcome."

He frowned at the way she balanced awkwardly. "You are still using the crutches."

"Yeah, it's the only way to keep up with Deefer. Is Kelmac around? I wanted to ask him something."

"He is in the chapel."

"OK, thanks." She turned, pausing as his hand closed on her arm. "What is it?"

"You are thinking of staying here when the others leave."

Lou frowned. That was a statement not a question. Was she that transparent? Or had her confidence been breached? She doubted anyone was reading her coded entries in the logbook and in any case, that would be Jim and no one else. "What if I am?"

"Do not lie to me. Keika said you spoke with her yesterday. You asked her to speak to Kelmac on your behalf. Why leave your friends to go on alone when you have come so far together?"

She sighed. "I know that I can't go with them. I have my reasons. I can't leave, so I need somewhere to stay. And I like it here."

He held her gaze. "Are you staying because of me?"

"Don't be silly. You're getting married. I know what that means. Besides, don't take it personally, but you're *way* older than I am." She spoke rapidly, her conscience barely even twinged at the lie. But then, lying had become second nature to her now. Despite not being as religious as the others, she'd tried to be good and tell the truth at first. But deception was far easier.

Actually it was kind of ironic. She hadn't been able to give the cops in Southampton, or even Jack Davies, the American she met in Cornwall, and who'd come to their aid more than once, most recently on Grand Turk, a false name when they'd asked.

But now, lying was simply water off a duck's back, easy as pie, as Jack would say. She wondered briefly what he was doing now. Presumably still working for the American government in whatever secret capacity he did.

"Those that do not eat cannot work and those that cannot work are no good to the community." Mafuso's voice jarred her back to reality.

She smiled at him. Trust him to bring her not eating into the conversation again. "I could help you with the medical bits or sew clothes or something." She changed the subject. "Anyway, you do realize you shouldn't see Tayba after sunset, and then not until the ceremony tomorrow."

He grinned at her. "That is a silly notion. Why ever not?"

"It's bad luck."

"There is no such thing as luck," Mafuso said firmly. "We make our choices and then follow the path God has set for us. Lou, you are still a child, on the verge of becoming a woman. Do not presume to know the path set out for you before you reach the signposts."

"I should go and find Kelmac." She turned to head across to the chapel.

"Will you be at dinner later?" he asked.

Lou didn't even pause. "Of course."

"Because if you stay, you will be back under my care, and you will have to eat and take care of yourself. The same as everyone else does. You will not heal if you do not eat."

Lou stopped and turned to face him. "Mafuso, we both know that's not true. I heard you, last night, first talking with Amilek, and then praying. I don't have many choices left, but this is one I will make for myself. I want to stay either here in the village, or somewhere on the island. I'd rather say goodbye to the others and wave them off, than have them..."

He gently took hold of her hand. "I understand."

"I wanted to stay anyway, but now it really is the only choice I have left. Please don't take it away from me."

"The decision is not mine to make. But I will speak to him for you if you wish."

"Thank you." She squeezed his hand and let go, moving slowly away. "C'mon, Deefer."

~*~

Jim jerked awake as someone splashed cold water on his face. "Hey!"

Staci flopped down beside him. "You're not getting any sympathy, so don't bother to ask," she said. "Wake up. I need to talk to you."

Jim groaned. "Go away."

"Fine," she huffed. "I shan't tell you."

"Tell me what?"

"You'll never know unless you wake up. And you've still got your eyes closed. Although you've spent most of the day sleeping, while everyone else has been working. Even Mafuso has been hard at it all day long."

Jim reluctantly opened his eyes. "OK. I'm awake. What do you want?"

"I want to go home," Staci said simply.

Jim sat bolt upright and stared at her, all traces of sleep gone. "You do?"

"Yes."

"Why?"

"It's nice and all here, but I've had enough now. I want to go back to school, where everyone speaks the same language as me and we can have proper dinners and I don't have to sleep on the floor or sew all day long. Even if Mum and Dad won't be there, I want to go home."

Jim smiled. "Sure, kiddo. I'll take you home. And if Mum and Dad don't come back, you won't have to go into care. I'm eighteen now. I'll take care of you."

"Jim, you've done a great job, but you can't do that from a ship or plane. You have wanted to join the navy or air force since forever. You can't put your life on hold for me any longer. I'll go to boarding school and spend the holidays with Nichola."

He hugged her. "All right. When do you want to leave?"

"Tomorrow," she said, hugging him back.

"That's the wedding. I thought you wanted to stay for that."

"I do. The day after tomorrow, then."

"I'll tell the others."

"OK. Thanks, bro."

"Anything for you, kiddo."

She smiled. "Besides, Lou needs to go home and see a proper doctor. Not that Mafuso isn't a proper doctor, but you know what I mean."

Jim nodded. "Yeah. He can only do so much." He pushed to his feet. "OK, I'm going for a swim, wake myself up. You coming?"

She nodded. "Race you over there." She tore across the clearing.

Jim followed her, deliberately letting his younger sister win. He'd talk to Ailsa later, over dinner perhaps. He hadn't known her long, but he didn't want to lose her. She'd become a huge part of his life and he wanted her to stay that way. Then that just left Lou. She was even more secretive than normal and that worried him. What was she planning? More to the point, could he stop her from doing it?

15

The small chapel was quiet. Lou stood in the doorway, watching Kelmac. Then she made her way inside. "May I speak with you?" she asked in a hushed whisper, not wanting to disturb the silence.

Kelmac turned and smiled at her. "What can I do for you?"

Now the moment was here, she hesitated. What if he said no? Then where would she go? She lowered herself onto a stool beside him. "The others are planning on leaving soon," she said quietly. "I would imagine pretty soon after the wedding, probably the following day. Jim wants to get Staci back to England, see if there is any news about their parents."

Kelmac nodded. "I presumed as much." He tilted his head, holding her gaze. "You do not wish to go with them."

"I—" she broke off. "How did you know? Has Keika already spoken to you? She said she would, but I wanted to before she did."

"You said *the others* are leaving. You did not say *we*. Therefore it is obvious that you are not planning to go with them."

"Oh." Lou rubbed her leg. She looked at the

ground. "No, I don't want to leave. I want to stay here."

"Why not go with the others? They are your family, are they not?"

"Close friends, not family. But I like it here."

Kelmac hardened his gaze. "Tell me, once Mafuso is joined to Tayba, will you like it as much?"

Lou's stomach lurched and her face burned. "Of course. I'm a child, according to him. Besides, he and Tayba are soul mates. Once they're married he's off limits, same as every other married man. Just like Jim is now because he loves Ailsa." She sucked in a deep breath. "You want the truth?"

Kelmac nodded. "The truth is always the best way. Even if it hurts."

She paused slightly. "You sound like my mother."

"Then your mother is a wise woman." He tilted his head. "You have never spoken of her to anyone. Is she still alive?"

"She, ummm, she's not dead. At least, I don't think so. My father is. It's just her and me."

"I don't understand. If you are all she has, then why not go home to her?"

Lou looked up. "Because I'm dying. I overheard Mafuso talking last night when he thought I was sleeping. I tried to let him believe that my leg was healing, that the pain was lessening, but it isn't and he wasn't falling for it. I'm cold and can't get warm, and my head hurts all the time. It's not fair of me to give the others false hope. Or, if we do get rescued, to do the same to Mum. For her to have lost me all these months, and get me back for a few days? A month, at the most? It's not fair. It's better if they think I've chosen to stay behind, than to go home just to die."

Kelmac's frown deepened. "So you would rather lie to them then tell them the truth? What about their choice in all this?"

"I'm trying to protect them. This way they'll think I've got a happy ever after and needn't know I only have a short time left." The tears she'd held in for so long trickled down her face. "Please…"

He shook his head. "I cannot let you do that to them. And I think, that no matter what you are feeling now, you would regret it if you didn't give them the chance to say goodbye."

"But they will," she insisted. "They just won't know I'm dying."

"If you stay, then you have to tell them the truth. And not lie to me about it, simply to get your own way." Kelmac stood, signaling the conversation was over. "I have made my decision. Now I have things to do for tomorrow."

"Sure." Lou slowly left the chapel and headed down to the river, Deefer running at her heels. Now what would she do? She slid to the forest floor and leaned against a tree.

At this point, Jim would usually pray. But she wasn't Jim. And anyway, why should she pray to a God who wanted her dead at sixteen? Ironic, in a way. She'd wanted to die just after the shark attack, and now she was going to, she wasn't sure about it at all.

~*~

January 10, day 51, dawn. The wedding. Lou writing.

It's already humid and hot, despite the fact the sun hasn't been up long. It's going to be a long day. The wedding ceremony itself is happening pretty early on, with the rest of the day being spent celebrating before Mafuso and Tayba leave to go to their new house and are left alone for the evening.

Jim is planning on leaving at first light tomorrow. He says that way we can make a good start towards the coast and where he thinks this base is.

.gniog ton ma I... I don't care what anyone says, I can't go with them. I'll go as far as the base and then when rescue arrives, I shall take my leave. Deefer and I will find somewhere else to live. There must be another village or something. Or we just find a nice shady tree to sit under and wait for the inevitable. I will meet death on my terms... ecoihc yM

I better get up. Everyone else has. Mafuso looks nervous. For once it's him complaining he's not hungry. It is so tempting to tell him if he doesn't eat he'll get sick, but I don't think he'd find that funny. Don't think anyone would today. It's meant to be a happy occasion, but there is a great lack of smiles and laughter this morning.

OK, the men have left. That's our cue to get changed into the formal robes they've provided for us.

Lou put the pen down and closed the book.

She reached for the clean robe that Ailsa had laid out for her. She shivered and pulled the robe on over the one she already had one. Perhaps the double layer would help warm her up.

Staci smiled. "That color suits you."

"Not as much as that one suits you, Stace." She slowly pulled herself to her feet and looked at the untouched plate of food beside her. "I might give breakfast a miss. Not feeling so good and I don't want to ruin the day by throwing up."

"Mafuso said…"

"He didn't eat either, did he?"

Staci shook her head. "No."

"And I suppose you're still hungry."

"Of course."

"So you eat mine and then everyone's happy."

"You will eat something later though, right?"

Lou forced a smile. "Of course. I'm looking forward to that cake thing Keika made."

As the sun rose fully above the trees, a drum began to sound.

Everyone assembled at the center of the village, by the raised dais.

Kelmac stood there, with his full ceremonial headdress on. Feathers and beads cascaded over his shoulders and his long, blue cloak reached the ground.

The drumbeat increased and then stopped.

Music floated over the village as Sivelle led Tayba out towards the dais.

Keika played a wooden flute.

The music first scaling high, then low

brought a lump to Lou's throat. This was something she'd never do. She wouldn't even see Jim or Staci get married. Staying here would be easier on her than anyone else if she were honest.

Tayba's dress was yellow-gold. It floated down from her shoulders, hardly touching her at all, before it reached the ground. Her hair was hidden under a veil of blue, which was also floor length. She looked radiant.

The drums started up again, as the women began to sing.

Lotho took Tayba's hand and led her onto the dais.

Kelmac offered him a knife and as the singing rose, Lotho cut one of the cords from his robe and used it to tie Tayba's wrist to Mafuso's. This symbolized him giving his daughter freely in marriage. He returned the knife to Kelmac and returned to Sivelle.

The singing, music and drums ceased.

Kelmac raised his hands and held them over Mafuso and Tayba. He chanted slowly and quietly, yet in the hush that had descended over the whole village, every word was audible. As Kelmac chanted, his voice rose and fell almost rhythmically. As the ceremony progressed, Tayba knelt. Kelmac cut the cord on her wrist and handed her a bowl of water.

Tayba took the bowl and poured the water over Mafuso's feet, symbolizing her devotion and obedience to him.

Kelmac then raised the knife over Tayba and brought it down, as if to kill her.

Mafuso grabbed his wrist and pointed the knife towards himself, declaring that he would give his life for Tayba's. Mafuso raised Tayba to her feet.

Kelmac chanted a final blessing and Mafuso took his new wife into his arms and kissed her.

The drums and music started up again and all the villagers began singing.

Deefer barked and dashed around madly.

Lou grabbed his collar. "Shh, you daft dog. Sit down. You're spoiling it." She pulled the camera from her pocket and took a couple pictures.

After a while, the singing finished and the bride and groom stepped off the dais to a sea of congratulations.

The celebrations began with a feast and then dancing which continued well into dusk.

Towards the end of the evening, Kelmac raised his hands for silence. "Tonight we celebrate the union of Mafuso and Tayba. We celebrate life and love and friendship. Tomorrow we must say goodbye to friends. Jim, Lou, Staci, and Ailsa will be leaving us to continue their long journey home." He turned and looked at them. "You have been true friends. You helped rebuild the village after the fire. Helped us, who were total strangers to you. Jim, you saved my son's life. You have taught us about your culture and in return have learnt about ours. You have given us as much as we have given you. You have enriched our lives by coming to us."

Jim stood up. "As you have enriched our

lives," he replied. "You took a huge risk when you asked us to stay. You had little left after the fire, but helped us anyway. Took us in. Clothed and fed us. Thank you for having us here for so long. We have all enjoyed living with you for the past couple of weeks. We will cherish our memories of this time together for the rest of our lives."

As Jim sat down, Staci said, "I never realized you were so eloquent, bro."

"Nice speech, Jim," Lou told him.

"Thank you." Jim smiled, his smile growing as Ailsa slid her hand into his.

Mafuso and Tayba stood by the dais, talking to some of the other villagers.

Lou made her way over to them. "Thank you for letting us share today with you," she said.

"Thank you for all you have done," Tayba said. "You have all given us far more than we gave you."

Lou gave Tayba a hug and after a pause gave Mafuso one too. "Be nice to each other," she said and returned across to where Ailsa was waiting for her.

They returned to Amilek's hut for the last time. "I feel so much at home," Lou said as they sat down to eat the light supper of fruit. "I don't want to leave."

"You are coming, though," Ailsa said sharply.

"I said I would. It's a joint decision. You go, we go."

"Good."

Jim glanced over at Amilek. "Do you know anything about the journey between here and the coast?"

"The American base?"

"Yes. Have you been there?"

"Many years ago. It is a three-day walk from here at a normal pace, but I would expect it to take you a week at the pace Lou walks. The beach itself is just beyond the buildings." He paused. "Do you wish me to come with you?"

Jim shook his head. "Thank you for the offer, but we will be fine."

Amilek nodded. "If you do not find a way home, you are all welcome to return and make your home here with us."

"Thank you."

Lou glanced up at Keika, and then back down.

Jim touched her arm gently. "Something bothering you?"

She shook her head. "Just tired. Been a long day. I might lie down and write all this up in the logbook."

"OK."

She made her way over to her mat and pulled the logbook from under her pillow. Starting with the mirror writing, she wrote. *.riafnu oS I can't stay on my own, but everybody else can. The point of staying when they weren't was...oh, forget it. I'll come up with another plan ...ebyaM*

Anyway, on to the wedding. I took a couple of pictures and hopefully they can go in here at some point.

~*~

In the morning they packed their few belongings into Lou's waterproof bag.

Keika gave them each a new set of clothes, which Jim packed carefully along with the logbook and camera.

After breakfast they went across to say thank you and goodbye to Kelmac. When they came out the whole village had gathered to see them off.

Mafuso handed them a huge bag. "Food," he said. "It should take a week to reach the coast. There is food here for ten days. Also medicine for Lou. Try to get her to take it."

"Thank you," Jim said. "I'll try, but you know how stubborn she can be."

Kelmac handed him a spear. "In case you have need of it."

Jim took it. "Thank you." He shouldered the two bags. "Time to be off, ladies," he said.

Another round of goodbyes began and they finally set off, with Deefer bounding down the path on his lead.

16

They followed the path away from the village moving slow for Lou's sake.

Deefer tugged at his lead, eager to be free to explore.

"No, Deefer!" Lou told him, after he almost pulled Staci over. "You stay on the path."

Deefer barked in annoyance, but did as he was told.

They journeyed on, following the path. By lunchtime, they had walked for three and half-hours. Lou was struggling to keep up, but determined not to say anything. A three day journey would take them at least six if not longer.

When they stopped, Ailsa took some bread out of the bag and some of the fruit.

Lou took the fruit and nibbled it slowly. She laid the bread on her lap and glanced at Staci, then down at the bread, indicating she could have it.

Staci finished hers and deftly grabbed Lou's bread, biting it before anyone could say anything. "You know, as much as I've enjoyed staying in the village and being around other people, it is nice to be on our own again."

"If you say so," Lou said, rubbing her leg.

"Did we bring the splints?"

"Yeah why? Is it hurting again?" Jim reached into the bag. "Here."

"Too much exercise I guess. I'll be fine." She took the splints and strapped them on, easing the pain considerably. "That's better."

Jim said, "We need to move on again. Amilek said the base is a three day walk away, and we have food for ten days. If we do it in three days, it means six hours walking a day—at least. Are you all up to that?"

"Yes," Staci and Ailsa answered.

Jim looked at Lou. "Lou?"

"Yes." She avoided his gaze. "But I'd rather we aimed for five days. I mean, we've been on Agrihan fifty-two days now. What's a few more?"

Jim nodded. "Fair enough, but can you keep up?"

"If I take double doses of the mytona or Mafuso's equivalent, then I can keep up just fine. Starting from now."

He handed over the bottle. "But I want to keep hold of it."

"Don't you trust me?" she demanded. "Jim, why would I want to take all of it at once and risk running out?" She tightened her grip on the bottle. "This way I can take it when I need it. Please?"

He nodded, concern and reluctance in his gaze. "OK. Right, then. Let's go."

"Look out England. Here we come!" Staci said.

They walked another four hours that

afternoon, with Lou taking sips of the mytona when she didn't think anyone was looking.

Finally Jim called a halt and they camped by the river.

Staci closed her eyes. "I'm too tired to miss the bed I slept on for the last couple of weeks. Don't even want to eat."

Jim looked at her. "Are you sick?" he asked.

"Nope. Just tired." She tilted her head. "I can be sick and tired if you want."

He tossed a piece of fruit at her. "I'd rather you not be sick. So eat this with your eyes closed."

Deefer took the guard position at Lou's feet. He was more protective of her now she had left the safety of the village.

Lou stroked his head as she curled up on her side. "Daft dog," she said. "What would I do without you?"

~*~

For three days they walked and followed the path away from the village towards the coast.

Even with the mytona, Lou was struggling to keep up. She had twisted her left ankle badly the previous evening. It had torn open the old wounds. She said nothing to the others, and treated it herself.

They needed to get to the base and get hold of someone to pick the others up.

Jim called a rest break.

Lou sank gratefully to the ground, rubbing

her knee. After lunch she pulled herself up. "We should be going," she said.

"Already?" Jim asked. "What's the rush?"

"You wanted to get there in a week. It's still at least two days. Let's go."

"You're in pain. You need to rest."

Lou glared at him. "You give it a rest! You can catch me up." She shook her head and headed off as fast as she could on her crutches.

"Stay on the path," he called after her.

Deefer bounded after her, barking.

~*~

Jim pushed to his feet and picked up his pack. "Better go after–"

A scream interrupted him and then a shrieking yowl that made his blood run cold.

Both Ailsa and Staci stood, eyes wide with fear.

"What was that?" Staci whispered.

Jim hurtled at breakneck speed down the path.

Ailsa and Staci were right on his heels.

"Lou!" he shouted. "Lou, where are you?"

"Here," came an agonized reply. "Please come quickly."

"Where?"

"Off the path to the right. Please Jim. Hurry." Lou sounded desperate.

Jim pushed through the brush.

Lou was on her knees on the ground, her hands covered in blood.

Deefer lay by her side whimpering and thrashing.

Jim stopped short. "Are you OK?"

Horrified gasps came from the girls.

Lou looked up, tears pouring down her face. "He pushed me out of the way. I fell. He ran straight into it. I can't free him. Help me please."

Jim dropped to his knees.

Deefer was moaning, his eyes rolling as he tried to free himself. One of the large metal traps pressed into him, holding him fast around his middle.

Lou was holding the dog in place as she sobbed. "I was headed straight for it. He pushed me aside. I can't get him out."

"I can, give me a second." Jim quickly freed Deefer.

Ailsa gently examined the dog. "He's badly mangled. Let's get him back to the river and I'll bathe and dress it."

"You can't move him," Lou objected.

"We have to." Jim gently scooped Deefer up and carried him back towards their bags.

Deefer licked Jim's face, twisting in his arms to try to get to the mangled stomach.

"Hold still, boy," Jim soothed, squeezing the dog to hold him firmly. "We'll soon have you back to rights." But even as he said it, he feared the worst.

~*~

Staci helped Lou up.

When they reached the others, Ailsa had filled a bowl with water and was attempting to bathe Deefer's wounds.

Deefer, like any wounded animal, growled and snapped, not letting her anywhere near it.

Lou took the cloth. "Let me try," she said. She got down beside her injured companion and stroked him gently. "Hey, boy. Can I see?"

Deefer whined and covered it with his paws.

Lou said, "Please? Why did you do it? Why push me aside like that? Let me help you now, yeah?"

Deefer looked up at her, pain and trust etched in his eyes. He let her move his paws.

Lou's eyes filled with tears again. It looked worse now they were in the clearing.

"Silly animal, aren't you, eh? Let me clean it, OK? Then Ailsa will bandage it to keep it clean."

Deefer moaned as she washed the wound out, only half-heartedly snapping at her once.

As Ailsa gently wrapped strips of cloth around his injury, Lou stroked him.

He closed his eyes.

Ailsa looked at Lou. "See if he'll take some of the mytona from you."

Lou poured a little into her hand and persuaded Deefer to drink it. He closed his eyes again and sighed. She sat with him, rubbing his head and talking to him.

"Let him sleep Lou," Ailsa said. "He needs to rest."

She looked up. When had it gotten dark? "OK."

~*~

"Staci's made dinner. Come and have some."

Lou looked around.

Jim had made a fire, ringed by stones as he'd been taught in the village.

Ailsa carefully moved Deefer over to the fire.

Lou sat next to him and Jim pressed a cup into her hand.

"Drink this," he told her.

"Don't want it."

"Drink it," he ordered. "You have to."

Lou looked at him. "Jim, what if he dies?"

"He'll be fine. You'll see. Now drink up."

"OK." Lou drank slowly, not taking her eyes off Deefer. That night she lay next to him, hardly sleeping at all. The log book on her lap, she wrote a tear stained entry.

January 13, day 56, Lou writing. Deefer's hurt and it's my fault. Jim told me to wait and I didn't. He wanted me to rest and I didn't. He told me to stay on the path and I didn't. If I had, then Deefer wouldn't have followed me and he'd be OK. Now he's really badly hurt. One of those trap things dug its evil teeth into him and…

Without him, I'm nothing. He's been the one constant in my life. The only one who stands up for me no matter what, the only one who sits quietly and listens to whatever I say, and now, he could die because of what I did. Because I was stupid and didn't do as I was told and he saved me…

Deefer slept, whimpering occasionally.

When she finally did sleep, Lou dreamt about *Avon*. She dreamt they found a lake that wasn't on any map. *Avon* was moored to one side of it. She climbed aboard to find the boat full of unfriendly natives who wanted to sacrifice her to the volcano god.

Deefer chased them away, leaving the boat empty. Then she was back on the lakeside, watching the boat sink. She called Deefer's name.

An answering bark came from the boat. Lou watched in horror as Deefer stood on the deck, a bloodstained bandage around his middle, and went down with the boat.

She woke crying. It was morning and she was cold. She turned over to check Deefer. He wasn't there. She sat up and looked around wildly. "Where's Deefer?"

Staci smiled. "Jim took him for a walk."

"He *what*?"

"They'll be back soon. Are you hungry?"

"A little. What's the time?"

"Nearly eleven."

"Eleven?" Lou repeated.

Ailsa laughed. "Yeah."

"In that case, forget breakfast. I'll wait for lunch. Is Deefer OK?"

"He's fine. His usual bouncy self." As she spoke, Jim and Deefer came back.

Deefer charged over to Lou and covered her in licks.

"Hey, boy." she said, laughing as she petted and ruffled his fur. "Are you OK today?"

Deefer woofed. He sat next to her. His

middle was heavily bandaged. The bandage was bloodstained, but not as much as she'd expected.

Jim saw her looking and said, "He wanted to go for a walk," he told her. "It wasn't my idea. He needs to rest. I suggest we stay here today and move on tomorrow."

"So long as Deefer can keep up with us."

"Lou, I had to run to keep up with him."

~*~

January 14, day 57, Lou writing.

Is it really only a day since I last wrote in here? Deefer seems better today. Jim wants to rest, but Deefer doesn't. He keeps heading over to the path and then back to us. I don't want to go, but...no not even going to think it.

Jim writing now. Finally, I gave in and we set off towards the coast once we'd eaten something. Deefer kept up well. Too well, in fact, and we went further than I anticipated. Lou seems more willing to keep moving while he does.

When they camped that night Ailsa changed the dressings. "It looks infected. Maybe we should slow down and let him rest."

Jim nodded. "Might be an idea. We'll take tomorrow as a rest day. I can't see Lou arguing if we say it's for Deefer and not her."

Ailsa washed her hands and sat next to him. "She needs the rest just as much."

Jim sighed. "I know." He gazed into the fire. "I've prayed so hard, but..."

"Then let's do it again," she whispered,

laying her head on his shoulder.

~*~

January 15, day 58, Lou writing.

Didn't sleep. Deefer's stomach smelt overnight and when Ailsa changed the dressings it was obvious why. She was right. It's infected. Why did he do it? That trap was meant for me and he ran straight into it in my place.

"We have to stay here today, Jim," Lou said.

Jim looked at her. "I wasn't planning on going anywhere today. I agree with you that he needs the rest."

Deefer ran to the edge of the clearing and looked back at them. He returned to Lou and tugged at her.

Staci watched him. "I think Deefer has other ideas."

Jim said, "I think you're right. It's as if he wants us to go on."

"Well, we can't," Lou insisted.

Deefer barked and grabbed the edge of her robe, tugging harder.

She shook her head. "No. We're staying here. Jim, tell him."

"He's not listening, Lou." Jim stood. "Maybe we should go while he has the energy and rest when he does."

"Fine," she muttered. She shoved the logbook into the bag and handed it to Jim.

They packed up and set off again. Once more with Deefer leading them, they travelled further and faster than Jim had planned.

Jim commented to Ailsa, "We've more than made up for the time we lost. It's almost as if he knows where he's going."

"Maybe he does."

"How?"

"Sixth sense?" Ailsa suggested. "Or another reason he's not telling us."

Staci rolled her eyes. "He's a dog. In case it escaped your notice, he can't talk."

They made camp in a clearing by a stream.

Lou again sat up with Deefer all night.

He was weaker now, not even having the strength to wag his tail.

"You did too much," she told him. "We'll stay here tomorrow." When she did finally doze, she had the same nightmare.

17

January 16, day 59, daylight. Lou writing.

Everyone is up and about. I'm sat with Deefer. He doesn't want to move this morning. Don't blame him. We came too far the past few days. Too far and too fast.

Jim came over to her a big grin covering his face. "Morning. Guess what?"

"What?"

"Go to the edge of the clearing and see for yourself."

Lou grabbed her crutches and went to the tree line. The sea glinted just below them and a path wound down the cliff towards a series of buildings. She turned to look at her dog.

Deefer was lounging off to one side, probably hoping for a tidbit to be thrown his way.

"He led us here," she said wonderingly. "He somehow knew this was what we were looking for...perhaps he sensed something he was insistent that we come this way."

"I've heard of dogs doing extraordinary things like this before." Jim gazed at Deefer, too. "It's as if he knew we needed to find help in some way, and he just went about it."

Lou went over to Deefer, settling down beside him.

Deefer's tail thumped on the ground as he plopped his head in her lap. She petted her amazing hound, still bemused by his exuberance yesterday as he led them to this spot. Her mind wandered into nothingness as she pondered the base below. A head butted against her hand and she resumed stroking the dog's fur.

"Well," said Jim. "Since Deefer is the hero of the day, we'll have to give him a little extra food tonight."

Ailsa looked up. Comprehension dawned on her face. "He led us here."

Jim nodded.

"You're a good dog, Deefer." Staci reached across Lou's lap and patted his head. "But then, we always knew that."

The three of them exclaimed over Deefer's heroic deeds, with Staci reminiscing about other antics the dog had done when they were at home.

Ailsa listened, smiling as Staci got more excited with Deefer's exploits; laughing as she recounted the dog overboard incident on the boat.

Lou's mind returned to her melancholy thoughts. She was so tired. Every step today had been torture, the crutches digging under her arms, the nearly useless leg not cooperating in any way. Her heart...no, her soul...was just so weary.

She rubbed behind Deefer's ears, just the way he liked it. "Hey boy, we're almost there. Journey's end."

Deefer opened one eye and whimpered softly. He settled his head further onto her lap and sighed.

She stroked his head. "Not far now, Deefer. Just down the cliff path and then we can call for help. Find someone to make you better."

Deefer sighed again. He no longer had the energy to move. He looked up at her, the familiar look of love and trust in his eyes. He licked her hand.

Lou stroked behind his ears, tears filling her eyes. "You rest now, Deefer. You did well to lead us here. We'll explore the beach after lunch. You'll like that. Walk on the sand and run in the waves. Just the two of us, like we used to do on holiday."

Deefer closed his eyes and sighed as she stroked him.

His breathing became slower and more labored, until it finally stopped.

Lou sat for a while, unwilling to move and not wanting to speak just yet. Because once she did, she had to admit something she didn't want to.

After a while, she said, "Jim?"

Jim looked up from the logbook. "Yeah, what's up?"

"Come here a sec please."

Jim got up and came over. He sat next to her. "What is it?" he asked.

"It's Deefer," Lou whispered. She looked at him, tears streaming down her face. "He's..." she began, but got no further.

Jim put a hand on Deefer's chest. "He's gone," he said softly. "Oh, Lou. I am so sorry.

Come here." He gathered her in his arms and held her as she sobbed.

Staci and Ailsa came back from gathering fruit.

Ailsa looked at Jim. "What's up?" she asked.

"Deefer's dead," Jim replied softly.

"No." Staci began to cry. She dropped to the ground and buried her face in his fur.

Ailsa sat beside her and held her as they both cried, until they were exhausted and could cry no more.

Jim drew the others away and got them preparing the meat for that evening, while he went to a secluded spot by the cliff top. Later, he returned across to Lou. She still sat with Deefer's head in her lap. "Lou, we need to bury him," he said.

"No. I'm not going to leave him here."

"We have to bury him. He's gone, Lou. The bit that made him Deefer is no longer there. He got us as far as he could. We've gone much further than I thought we would in the last two days. He knew he was dying. He wanted to get us to the coast first."

Lou said sadly, "It should have been me. He died in my place. Why? It's not fair."

Unable to answer, Jim put a comforting hand on her shoulder and then left her alone. He crossed over to the others and shook his head.

Ailsa got up. "Let me try." She went over to Lou and sat beside her. "Lou, if we don't bury him, the wild animals will eat his body. Is that what you want?"

"No."

"Jim's dug a grave. He's chosen a spot overlooking the bay. It's time to let him go and say goodbye."

Lou nodded reluctantly.

Ailsa nodded to Jim and he came across with his spare vest. He began to wrap Deefer in it, but Lou stopped him.

"Use my other dress," she said. She pulled it out of the bag and gave it to Jim.

Jim wrapped the body and picking Deefer up gently, carried him across to the spot he had chosen.

Lou rose and she, Ailsa, and Staci followed Jim to the cliff top. He gently placed Deefer into the grave. Lou picked up a handful of dirt and sprinkled it in. The others too sprinkled a handful of dirt onto the body.

Jim, then, began to fill in the grave.

The sound of Lou's sobbing filled the air. "He was my friend. I failed him," she said.

As darkness fell, Jim lit the fire, and Ailsa began to cook the evening meal. Lou sat numbly by the graveside. When the meal was ready, Jim went over to her. "Time to eat," he told her.

"I'm not hungry."

"You have to eat."

Lou sighed. "Why? What's the point? He was my life, Jim. What am I going to do without him?"

"You carry on. He wouldn't want you to be sad. You cherish his memory and smile because he has lived. He brought us here, Lou. To journey's end. Tomorrow we go down to the base and call for help."

Jim held out his hand. "One step at a time, mate."

Lou grasped his hand and he helped her up, then let her settle closer to the fire.

Ailsa handed Lou a plate of food.

Lou shook her head. "I don't want it. I'm just so tired, and I don't feel like eating."

Ailsa shrugged and divided it up between the others.

Staci took a bite, her expression still alert and excited. "Action plan for tomorrow?"

"To the airbase," Jim answered. "See what radio equipment they left. Then wait, I guess. Why?"

"We're almost out of food. And I don't want to have to go find more."

Jim snorted. "I knew you'd have an ulterior motive. You and your stomach." He finished his dinner and looked at the others. "I would suggest a game, but there's only the firelight."

"Coward, since when has that stopped us?" Staci told him. "Afraid you'll lose more like. Deal the cards. Playing, Lou?"

"No. I'll just watch." Lou watched as Jim swiftly dealt the cards and they played by the fire. After the game, when the others were asleep, Lou lay awake, her heart still breaking silently within.

~*~

In the morning, Lou woke, not realizing she had slept. She wondered why she had this ache inside her, as she instinctively looked for Deefer. Then she remembered. Grief descended on her like a crushing blow and she felt sick.

Jim made to go over to her, but Ailsa grabbed his arm. "Leave her, Jim. She won't want an audience. Trust me. I've been there."

Jim nodded. "OK. We'll move out after breakfast." He smiled as Lou came across to them. "Hi. Sleep OK?"

She shrugged. "Must've slept, but I don't remember."

"We're going in a few. Suss out the base and go fishing."

Lou sat down, wincing slightly. "I'll stay here."

"Not an option. We go, you go."

"I'm not leaving Deefer."

Jim sighed. "You want something to eat?" he asked, changing the subject.

"I'm not hungry."

"You need to eat."

"Later then. If I eat now, I'll be sick again."

"Jim, leave it." Ailsa said sharply. "Just hand out the fruit, please. I can't cope with arguments this morning. I've only known Deefer a few weeks and I miss him. He's been part of Lou's life for years."

Staci wandered over. "Morning campers. What's for breakfast?"

"Fruit. If Jim ever gets around to doing it," Ailsa said.

Jim raised his hand in defeat. "OK."

Lou rose and limped off up the path, leaving

them to it. By the time they'd finished, she still hadn't come back, so they started to pack up camp.

"Where's Lou?" Jim asked when they were ready to leave.

Ailsa pointed across the clearing. "Over there."

"OK. You two start down to the base. We'll catch you up."

Jim went across to where Lou stood by Deefer's grave. She held his collar and lead in her hands. Jim stood silently next to her for a minute. "Lou. I'm really sorry. I was wrong to speak to you like that earlier, but I can't leave you here on your own."

Lou looked at him and Jim recoiled slightly, horrified by what he saw. Her eyes were dead. It was as if her very essence had been buried along with Deefer. "I'm not going," she said, her voice expressionless. "I killed him. I'll only do the same to you."

"I thought we'd sorted this out," Jim said infuriated with her. "Of course you're coming." He shouldered the bag. "You've got three minutes. Then I shall pick you up and carry you." He walked off towards the cliff path.

Lou resisted internally, but a sweeping blackness swallowed her heart. She felt as if she were drowning, as if nothing mattered anymore.

Jim stood, confident, unwavering, as he waited for her to make up her mind.

Lou swallowed, fighting the feeling of being wrapped in a dark, smothering sheet, struggling to break free. After several intense moments, something firmed up in her brain, shifting the black to a gauzy gray, as if there was a light shining in the far distance.

Lou grasped at it like a drowning victim clinging to a raft, and swung after Jim.

18

Outside the USAF base, Staci and Ailsa waited for the others to catch up.

The gates hung open and lopsided.

Staci sighed. "Doesn't look hopeful, does it, Ailsa?"

"Not really. More derelict than I thought it might be."

Jim came over. "Lou's coming, under protest. Don't make an issue out of it. I've already put my foot in it enough for now."

The others nodded as Lou caught them up.

"Nice place," Lou said, not bothering to hide the sarcasm.

The base was run down. Jim and the girls went through the gates and up to the main building. Several hangers were dotted around the complex, all with broken roofs. Weeds sprouted up through the paving and the flagpole was noticeably empty. The windows of the main building were covered in dirt.

Ailsa rubbed at one and peered in. "No one home," she said.

"Really? You don't say," Jim said pushing at the door. It didn't budge.

"Try the handle," Staci said. She pushed it

down and the door opened. "Works every time."

She led the way inside the main building. A layer of dust covered the reception desk. Jim ran his finger across it and said, "Remind me to have words with the cleaners."

Lou looked up from the floor plan she'd found. "Radio room is on the third floor. Reckon the lift works?"

Jim grinned. "If not, I'll carry you."

They made their way to the stairs and Lou slowly and painfully hopped up them.

On the third floor they found the radio room. It was empty. A couple of dust covered tables and a few sheets of paper were all it contained. Jim sighed. He hadn't expected to find a radio, but he had allowed himself to hope.

Lou limped to the window. She rubbed at it and peered through at the runway. She glanced over her shoulder. "They'd never land on that anyway. It's more holes than runway."

Jim, Staci and Ailsa explored the base a bit more. They were all disappointed at not finding a radio. That is all except Lou. She was pleased. Now she could stay with Deefer. She missed him so much nothing else mattered. She followed the others slowly through the empty rooms, their footsteps echoing.

She felt dreadful and it wasn't just grief. She was hot and dizzy. All she wanted to do was go to bed and stay there. Once the others had been picked up, she'd go and sit by Deefer's grave and wait for the end to come. It wouldn't be long, she knew that.

Staci wandered into a side room. "Jim, what's this?" she called.

Jim pushed the door open wider. "What's what?" he asked.

"This," she said pointing to the desk.

"Staci, you gem." Jim yelled and hugged her. "It's a cipher. Morse code. We can use it to call for help. My Morse is a little rusty, but I know enough to spell out where we are. Any suggestions?"

He sat down at the desk and they worked out a short message. Jim flexed his fingers and said, "Here goes nothing." He tapped out the message. "SOS Agrihan Air Base. Need help. Please respond." He added their names and a request for information about his parents. They sat there for half an hour, waiting for a response.

"Nothing," Lou said. "No one uses Morse code anymore."

"So why do it?" Staci yelled. "Why'd you get our hopes up, Jim?"

"Stop it." Ailsa said, putting a hand on Jim's shoulder. "Shouting at each other isn't going to help and it was worth a shot. It'll be dark soon. I suggest we stay here tonight at least. Try again in the morning."

A flash of lightning split the sky and rain splattered against the window. "Good idea," said Jim. "At least we'll be in the dry. There should be a mess and barracks here somewhere."

"Somewhere on this level will do for now. I can't do those stairs again," Lou said.

Ailsa divided the remaining food into eight

portions and gave them one portion each.

"Thanks for nothing," Staci muttered.

"Have mine," Lou told her. "I'm not hungry."

Jim shot her an angry look. "You haven't eaten all day, Lou."

"I don't feel very well. If I eat I'll be sick and that will be a waste of what little food we have. I'm going to find somewhere to sleep." Lightning flashed again, illuminating her pale face. Thunder echoed in response.

Jim glanced at Ailsa, trying to indicate he didn't want Lou left alone.

She seemed to know what he meant as she nodded almost imperceptibly. "I'll come with you. If we find a big enough room, the four of us can camp together."

The two of them left the room. Staci looked at Jim. "Sorry, bro."

Jim put his arms around her. "It's OK, kiddo. I'd got my hopes up too. We'll try sending again tomorrow. Someone will hear us."

Ailsa came back. "We found something," she said. "A bunk room with four bunks and blankets. It'll mean Jim sharing with us, but I think we can cope for a few nights. What about you Stace? Jim doesn't get a say in the matter."

"I see," Jim said. "Like that is it?"

Thunder resounded through the empty building, making Staci jump. "Please, Jim. I need you tonight. So does Lou. Although she won't admit it."

Jim sighed. "You really want me to share

with a bunch of women?"

Staci rolled her eyes. "You've done it for weeks. The only difference is we're inside and not outside."

"True. Sure, we can all bunk together. Is Lou all right, Ailsa?"

"Very quiet, which is only to be expected. She's already lying down and will be sleeping before long."

"I'm going to bed. Ailsa, where's Lou?" Staci asked.

"Third door on the right Stace. We'll be right behind you."

Staci ran down the corridor as the rain thudded against the window.

Jim looked at Ailsa. "I'm worried about Lou. You didn't see her up at the graveside. When she looked at me her eyes were empty. She scared me, Ailsa. There was nothing there. It was as if we'd buried her along with Deefer. I'm afraid she of what she might do."

"She's grieving. She'll be OK. Just give her some time."

"OK."

Ailsa hugged him. "We won't leave her alone. That way she can't do anything."

Jim held her gaze. "And I want the mytona out of her bag. Just to be on the safe side."

She frowned. "Do you really think she'd do that?"

"I'm praying she won't, but there is something going on with her. More than just grief for Deefer. I just don't know what."

Clare Revell

19

The next morning was sunny. The overnight storm had dispersed some of the humidity. Lou looked out of the window across the pot-holed runway to the sea. The sun glinted off the top of the waves making them sparkle. The others were still asleep, so she quietly limped across the room and opened the door.

"Where are you going?" Jim asked.

Lou jumped, not realizing he was awake. "Nowhere far."

Jim leapt off the top bunk and landed with a thud, waking the other two. "Good morning," he said loudly.

"Brat," Staci muttered, rolling over and tugging the blanket over her head.

"And good morning to you, too," Ailsa yawned.

Lou limped down the corridor and towards the stairs. She sat on the top one and sliding her crutches to the bottom, bumped herself down after them as a small child does.

"Let me help you," Jim said from above her.

Lou looked up at him, her empty gaze again filling him with horror. "I don't need your help. I can manage." She slid herself around to the top of the next flight and sent her crutches down them, before following them. She reached the ground floor and swung herself rapidly along the corridor. Running footsteps behind her made her slow down.

Jim caught her arm. "Lou, wait up. Where are you going?"

"Outside."

"No. I don't want you wandering off on your own."

"Why? Afraid I'll get lost? I don't need you to take care of me. I don't need it and I don't want it. I'm going back to Deefer. He doesn't like being alone."

Jim held her arm tighter. "After breakfast. Then you can go. The rest of us are going fishing on the beach. We only have enough food for breakfast."

"I don't have a choice, do I?"

"No, you don't. After you."

Lou sighed. "You seriously want me to go all the way back up those stairs and then back down again?"

"OK." Jim yelled up the stairs to the others. "We'll eat down here as soon as you lot get up."

"Two secs," Staci yelled back.

Lou slowly made her way down the corridor and sat on the steps of the building, gazing out over the sunlit base.

As the others joined her, Jim said grace.

Ailsa took the remaining four portions out of the bag and gave them one each.

Lou immediately gave hers to Staci, ignoring

a look from Jim that would have made anyone else eat it.

Staci finished eating. "If that was breakfast, roll on lunch."

Jim shook his head. "We've only just finished breakfast and you're talking about lunch."

"Well, I'm hungry."

"Well, there isn't any more," Lou said bluntly. "But I'm sure we'll manage. We always do."

Jim looked at the others. "I'm going to try the cipher again. Then, we're going fishing. Ailsa knows a thing or three about fishing. Lou's right, we'll manage. There's bound to be fruit around somewhere anyway."

"You go fishing; I'm going to sit with Deefer." Lou headed off, not giving the others a backwards glance.

Jim sighed.

"I've got the mytona," Ailsa told him. "Go and try the Morse code and we'll wait here for you."

Ailsa as it turned out, knew more than a thing or three about fishing. Between her and Jim, they caught enough for two meals. Staci alternated between watching them and building a sandcastle. Jim then built a fire on the beach. Ailsa baked half the fish in leaves and stewed the other half in some river water.

Just as it was cooked, and Ailsa had put out the fire, Jim heard a noise. He got to his feet and looked skyward. "Is that a plane?" he asked. "It is. Look."

A fighter shot over from behind them and circled around over the base. Jim waved madly to get its attention. The plane circled again then disappeared off into the distance without seeing them.

Staci's face fell. "We should have stayed on the base."

Jim shoved down his disappointment and the feeling that his sister was right. Hopefully they'd have seen the smoke from the fire and know someone was here. "They'll come back. I'll send another message as soon as we get back. I'll go and get Lou. Meet you at the base. You bring the fish up with you."

"Leave her, Jim," Ailsa said.

"She ought to eat. I also want to get some wood for tonight and tomorrow, so we can stay on the base."

Jim ran up the path past the airbase and into the forest. Lou was where he thought she'd be—sat by Deefer's grave. "I need your help." he panted, out of breath from having run so far.

"I'm no good at CPR, so don't drop dead at my feet."

"Oh ha, ha, ha. I need some wood taken down to the airbase. Lots of wood. Can you help?"

Lou glared at him. "How can I carry wood?"

"So go stay with Staci, and send Ailsa to help me please."

In answer, Lou got to her feet and swung herself off down the path.

Jim looked sadly at Deefer's grave. "We all

miss you boy, but I think you've taken your mistress with you."

That evening they sat in the mess hall, which they'd discovered on the second floor. As dirty and dusty as the rest of the building, as least it gave them tables to eat off. Lou as usual, gave Staci her portion. Jim didn't bother to argue this time.

Ailsa found some hurricane lamps and matches to light them with. "All the comforts of home," she said.

"Except the fish and chip shop," Staci said.

"You've had the fish, what more do you want, kiddo?"

"Chips. Preferably covered in salt and vinegar, wrapped in newspaper, with a wooden fork to eat them with and ice cold coke to drink. Followed by raspberry roulade with that squirty cream from the can."

Jim laughed. "Not me. I fancy pizza. Nine-inch deep pan with pepperoni, peppers, sweetcorn, pineapple, spicy beef and extra cheese. With ice cold orangeade."

"Yuk." Ailsa said. "I'm a burger person with lots of salad." She looked at Lou. "What do you fancy?"

"Nothing. Feel too sick to eat and thinking about food makes me feel worse. Sorry. I think I'll go to bed. See you in the morning."

She pushed her chair back and stood.

Jim got up. "I'll carry a lamp up for you. I want to resend the Morse signal a third time anyway." He picked up one of the lamps. "Won't be long," he told the others. On the third floor, they went first to the signals room. As they walked down the corridor he looked at Lou. She looked dreadful. "Are you OK?"

"Not really. I don't feel so good."

In the signals room, Jim resent the SOS message twice, this time adding the need for urgent medical attention for Lou.

Lou looked at him. "Do you really expect them to come?"

"A plane came over earlier and circled the base while we were on the beach. I plan to stay here tomorrow in case they come back."

~*~

January 19, day 62. Lou writing.

Jim's been up since five. He resent the SOS and then went outside and started a fire in a metal drum that Ailsa found. He seems sure this plane will come back. I hope it does. It means they can go home. At seven he woke the others, and was surprised to find me awake. Once I can stand I'm going up the cliff path to sit with Deefer. I'm pretty dizzy this morning and feel really sick.

~*~

Jim scanned the base compound for Lou. Ailsa stood at the fire and slowly added more wood to keep it burning. Staci, eager to help and added more wood to the pile Jim had made the previous evening. Ailsa tossed on another handful of wood. The smoke curled up into the perfectly blue sky. Seagulls swooped and called to each other.

Jim frowned and did another three sixty. "Where's Lou?"

"I'll give you three guesses, but you'll only need one," Ailsa said. "Shall I go after her?"

"Leave her. When she wants company she'll come find us—"

He broke off as a sudden roar came from behind them and a plane flew over the base. Staci and Jim waved frantically at it. The plane circled twice and dipped its wings.

Staci screamed. "It's seen us. It dipped its wings. It's seen us."

The plane flew lower as if inspecting the runway. Then a parcel dropped onto the runway and the plane banked, rose and disappeared.

Jim ran onto the runway and picked up the parcel. He ran back to the others and ripped it open, his hands shaking. A box was inside. He took the lid off, revealing several packets labeled MRE and sachets of juice and an envelope.

Jim handed the box to Ailsa and he ripped open the envelope.

He unfolded the letter and read it, his voice shaking.

"*Anderson AFB, Guam, Jan 19th. Dear Lou, Jim, Staci, and Ailsa, We received your distress signal and have noted your position. We assumed that you would be short of food and have enclosed some rations. We will send a helicopter to pick you up at 1100 hours. Please be ready to leave when the helicopter arrives.*

See you then. Colonel Jack Fitzgerald."

When he had finished there was silence.

Then Staci jumped up and down and screamed before hugging Jim tightly. "It's over. We're going home."

Ailsa looked at the sun. "It's only eight. We have three hours yet."

"Time for breakfast then," Jim said. "Courtesy of the United States Air Force."

Ailsa carried the box back inside and up to the mess hall.

Staci said, "Shall I get Lou?"

"No. We'll save her some," Ailsa said.

In the mess hall, Jim handed out the ration packs. They were all savory and dinner rather than breakfast, but a welcome relief from the fish and fruit. He poured the juice and they sat down to enjoy it.

Staci asked, "Do you suppose it's Lou's American guy, Jim? He was Jack Fitzgerald."

"Could be. Although there is bound to be more than one guy called Jack Fitzgerald in the States."

After they had finished, Jim looked at the others. "We ought to get organized. Could you two sort out in here? Put the stuff we used away and so on? Stace, make sure the logbook is in with Lou's sewing. I'd hate to leave anything behind."

"Sure."

"I'll go and get Lou. Tell her the good news." He stood up and set off to find Lou, knowing full well what her reaction to going home would be.

20

"No," Lou said for the fifth time. "I am not going home. I'm staying here."

Jim sighed. "At least come and say goodbye then. To Staci if no one else."

"No."

He waved his hands in despair. "All right then. Fine. Stay here. I give up." Jim turned and slowly stomped down the cliff path and through the gates into the base.

Staci looked expectantly at him. "Where is she?"

"She can't go as fast as Jim. She'll be here, Stace," Ailsa said. She could see how angry Jim was. He shot her a grateful look, as right now he couldn't think of a nice thing to say about Lou.

"It's really over, isn't it?" Staci said.

"Yes, kiddo. Our grand adventure, begun June first last year, ends today, January nineteenth. Two hundred and thirty-four days in all. Sixty-two of those spent on the island."

Staci thought for a minute. "Long time. Longer for Ailsa, though."

"I'm not going to miss it."

Jim looked at Ailsa in surprise. "Why not?"

"My parents died here. I'm hoping things

will be better now. And I'm also hoping that you guys will figure in my life somehow."

He hugged her tightly. "Try keeping me away. I don't intend to lose touch with you."

"That sounds good to me." Ailsa hugged him back.

Lou came down the cliff path and into the compound. "Looks cozy."

Jim smiled at her. "You came," he said, relief in his voice.

"To say goodbye. Nothing more." She limped over to Staci and hugged her. "I would write, but the post here is dreadful."

Staci pushed her away. "What do you mean say goodbye?"

"I'm not coming."

"Don't be silly," Staci said, tears filling her eyes. "You have to come."

Lou shook her head.

Staci began to cry, and Jim hugged her tightly.

"I can't go with you," Lou said. "I have to stay here. Please understand."

"I don't understand," Jim growled. "All I can see is how much you are hurting others. Which is more than can be said for you. It's a shame you can't. Go on then. Just go. Get out. We'll be better off without you."

Lou swung herself slowly until her back was towards them, and headed back to the gate.

"Jim," Staci sobbed. "What do we do? We can't go back without her."

"I don't know, kiddo. They'll be here soon.

Maybe they can talk sense into her."

"Maybe."

Jim stood quietly, holding his sister, his mind going over their long voyage. The explosion in the docks, La Palma, the hurricane, Grand Turk, and the shipwreck. And Deefer.

The silence was punctuated by Staci's sobs.

What had seemed like such a good idea after the earthquake and tsunami in May, had turned into an unmitigated disaster. Trying to find his parents had solved nothing. His boat was destroyed, Deefer had died, and Lou may as well have. She had shut them out of her life for good. He looked down at his sister. "You OK, Stace?"

"No. I don't want to leave without her."

The sound of helicopter blades filled the air. They looked up as the big Air Force helicopter swooped in low over the base and set down gently on the runway. The rotors slowly ground to a halt. Four officers in flight suits jumped out and crossed over to them.

Jim watched nervously. Now the moment of their deliverance was at hand, he was afraid. He knew there were consequences and repercussions to be faced because of their actions, and right now he didn't want to face them.

The pilot removed his mirrored shades and hooked them over the pocket of his flight suit. He smiled. "Hi, there."

"Jack." Staci said. She let go off Jim's hand and ran over to Jack. She hugged him.

"Hello, Staci," Jack smiled, returning the hug. He turned to his crew. "My crew, navigator/engineer Sergeant Murdoch, medic Captain Stevens and co-pilot Major Corrigan. This is Jim and Staci Kirk."

Jim shook Jack's hand. "It's good to see you again."

"The signature on the note," Staci said. "Colonel Jack Fitzgerald. Is that you?"

"At your service." He turned to Ailsa. "I don't believe we've met."

"Ailsa Cudby."

"Pleased to meet you." Jack's gaze took in the entire area. "Where's Lou and the dog?"

Staci's eyes filled again. "She's…she's not…"

Jack's piercing gaze swung back to them. "She's not what?" he asked, punctuating every single word.

Jim grabbed his sister's hand and squeezed it. He tried to comfort her, despite the distress and pain filling him. "It's OK, Stace."

"No, it's not." She looked at Jack. "Lou isn't coming."

Jack raised an eyebrow. "*Excuse me*?"

Staci took a deep breath. "Deefer died three days ago. We got shipwrecked in November and met up with Ailsa then. She's been here years. Deefer got caught in a trap, one of those metal ones. His wound got infected, and he died."

Jack fixed his piercing eyes on Jim. "I think it's time for the truth now, don't you? You haven't been on holiday at all, have you?"

"No," Jim admitted. "We left England to try to find my parents after they got caught up in the Philippines tsunami and declared missing. Only we ended up getting lost ourselves."

"I wanted to stay with Jim," Staci added. "Don't blame him, please. Lou and I stowed away to be with him. He didn't know about it until it was too late."

Jim looked at Staci. "I should have known better, Stace. I should never have let it happen."

"The wreck of your boat was found at the beginning of December some distance from here. There has been a huge search and rescue operation going on, looking for you three. Speaking of Lou, you didn't answer my question. Where is she?"

Jim, Staci and Ailsa looked at each other, neither willing to admit it. The silence was deafening.

"Where is she?" Jack repeated, his voice like thunder.

"Like Staci said, Lou says she isn't coming," Ailsa said eventually.

Jack raised an eyebrow. "Oh?"

"She's ill," Jim said. "She's not thinking straight."

Major Corrigan said, "Is that who the medical attention was needed for?"

"Yes. She got attacked by a shark in September and badly hurt her leg. It's probably infected again. She's been in agony for days, but is too stubborn to admit it." He then told Jack about how down Lou had been. "Since Deefer died, it seems to have come back," he concluded. "She's changed. There is no getting through to her. She scares me now. I'm worried about her.

She hasn't eaten for days as it is."

Jack looked worried. "Where is she? And don't make me ask again."

"On the beach. Out the main gates, turn right and follow the path. You can't get lost."

Jack nodded. "I'll go find her. We're taking you back to Anderson. There are some people there waiting anxiously to see you."

"Nichola," Jim guessed.

Jack grinned. "And your mom and dad."

Staci screamed, as Jim caught his breath. *"What?"* he managed.

"They got back to England in September. They'll tell you all about it themselves, but they are fine and can't wait to see you."

Jim hugged Staci tightly, his sister jumping up and down in his arms and squealing. "I don't believe it…"

Jack turned to his co-pilot. "Help them pack out of here, Major. I'll go round up the strays. You two get the chopper ready to go."

"Aye, sir."

Jack ran out of the gate and down the path that led to the beach.

21

Lou sat on the sand, looking out at the sea. Her crutches lay beside her. She had Deefer's lead in her hand. Tears rolled silently down her face. She couldn't leave him here on his own. She couldn't go home. She had no choice. There was no way out that she could see. Despite the warmth of the sun, she shivered with cold. Alone in the darkness of the tunnel, the only light was that of the oncoming train, getting closer and closer.

Jack stood and watched her for a minute or two. He slowly walked across the sand and positioned himself so that his shadow fell across her. Lou didn't appear to notice. "Looks like you could do with a friend," he said. "Or at least a shoulder to cry on." He sat down next to her and handed her a tissue.

Lou ignored it.

"Don't I even get a hello?" he asked.

Silence. He shook his head. "Jim was telling me about your fight with the shark. How's your leg?"

Lou responded for the first time. "Hurts."

"Can I have a look?"

"If you want," Lou said, not bothered one

way or the other. She hitched up her skirt.

She heard Jack's sharp intake of breath and glanced at her leg. She had to concede it did look nasty again. She had given up with the splints. All Mafuso's hard work had been undone.

The skin that first Jim and then Mafuso had tried to piece together was splitting and pus oozed from gaping sores. The bones grated painfully every time she moved. Her foot was white and cold to the touch, the up side of this being she could no longer feel it.

She shivered again and rubbed her arms. She was so cold and tired.

Why wouldn't they just leave her alone?

It wouldn't be long now and she'd be with Deefer.

Jack looked away from the damaged limb and looked at Lou. "You need to get that seen to ASAP."

Lou sighed. "Why?"

"Because looking at it and at you, the infection has spread. If it goes untreated it will kill you."

"I already know I'm dying. Tell me something I don't know," Lou muttered. "The sooner I die the better."

Jack grabbed her and turned her towards him. "Don't you dare talk like that. You're what, sixteen? C'mon tell me. What is so bad that you don't wanna see seventeen?"

Lou looked away and refused to answer.

Jack shook her slightly. "Talk to me," he ordered.

"I can't," Lou said. "And I'm not going home either."

"And why's that?"

"Which part of I'm dying don't you understand? I won't put the others through that. They've lost enough already. Better they think I'm alive and well here than watch me die like Deefer did."

Jack grasped her face in his hands and forced her to look at him. "We have just flown several hundred miles to rescue you. Your mom is on Guam waiting for you—waiting anxiously I might add. It was all I could do to stop her from insisting she came in the chopper with us. We are taking you home."

"No." Lou pulled herself free and struggled to her feet. "Leave me alone," she cried. "I'm staying here." She grabbed her crutches and limped away as fast as she could.

~*~

Jim stood with the others as the radio attached to the major's flight suit crackled.

"Sam, come in."

"Here, sir. Are you ready to go?"

"We got a problem. It's gonna take longer than I'd hoped. Fly the others out of here. First radio the base and have them send a life flight now."

"Sir?"

"Get a chopper sent out now. I want Doc Andrews on the flight. Tell her to bring IV antibiotics and have the base operating room standing on my return."

"Are you sure you want us to leave you here?"

"You have to. Shove the med kit in my flight bag. Leave that and the thermos on the runway."

"Sir, shall I leave Stevens with you?"

"No, you need a minimum crew of three. Go."

"Aye, Sir. See you back at base."

Jim heard her order the second flight, a life flight. How bad was Lou? He looked at the major as she turned around. "Is Lou not coming?"

"We're going on ahead. Colonel Fitzgerald will stay here with your friend. They've already gotten orders and a second chopper's on the way for them." She opened the helicopter door and Jim, Staci, and Ailsa climbed in the back. Stevens and Murdoch strapped them in, while Corrigan started the preflight.

Murdoch gave them headsets. "These are so we can communicate," he said. "It gets pretty noisy in here."

Jim looked around. "This is pretty big for a chopper. How fast can it go?"

Murdoch answered, "It can carry a crew of four and eight fully armed and loaded combat soldiers. It flies at a hundred eighty knots. It carries approximately five hours fuel and is able to be refueled in the air, but should not be flown for more than twelve hours with refueling."

Stevens laughed. "Quoting from the manual again?" The engine started and the rotors began to turn.

Staci slid her hand into Jim's. He squeezed it. The helicopter lifted up off the ground and into the air. "Bye, island," Staci said. "Bye, Deefer. See you soon, Lou."

The helicopter turned and flew over the beach before swinging out over the ocean. "How long is the flight?" Jim asked.

"Just over an hour," Corrigan answered.

"I hadn't envisaged going back without Lou," Jim said.

"Colonel Fitzgerald will bring her."

The chopper lifted off. Jim watched as Agrihan disappeared behind them. He wasn't happy about leaving Lou behind. Apparently, she was a lot sicker than she had let on. Why else had she been cutting them off the way she had been? If he hadn't been able to get through to her, how would someone she barely knew, succeed where he had failed, and persuade her to come home?

He pulled the log book from the bag and looked up. "I don't suppose you have a mirror, do you?"

Murdoch nodded and passed one over to him.

"Thanks." Jim flipped back a few pages in the log book and angled the mirror over Lou's coded entries.

I'm dying. Mafuso reckons there is nothing he can do. Not that he told me that. He insisted I was fine and healing nicely. I overheard the conversation with Amilek and when I confronted him, he didn't deny it. The infection is too deep, it's beyond his medical knowledge and we'll never get rescued in time. I've always known I'd never recover from this. That's why I'm not leaving Agrihan. I'll go with the others to the base and then come back here to the village and spend my last few days on our island in the sun. It's for the best.

Jim, when you eventually read this, forgive me. I didn't want you to know, because I hate goodbyes. I love you, I always have. Tell Stace I love her too. Take care of her. And tell Mum...

Tell her I love her and I'm sorry.

Jim closed his eyes, the vibration of the helicopter thudding through him. His stomach pitted and a spear plunged deep into his heart. His eyes burned beneath the lids and he turned his face away from the others.

He'd never see her again. The decision he'd made in September to take Lou fishing as punishment, the one he'd made in anger over her drawing all over the log book, would result in him losing his best friend.

Free Book Offer

We're looking for booklovers like you to partner with us! Join our team of influencers today and receive at least one free eBook per month. Maybe more!

For more information
Visit http://pelicanbookgroup.com/booklovers
or e-mail
booklovers@pelicanbookgroup.com